「用語道地，又像一幕幕愛情劇情節，很想知道接下來呢？接下來呢？學英語能夠這樣吸引你，聶雲這本書像一輩子心儀的情人，讓你愛上英文永不悔。」

暢銷英語書作家、文學作家
成寒

「一翻開聶雲的書，看到許多鮮活幽默的對白，真是有趣極了！學英文就是要從真心想學開始，用談戀愛的心情學英文，很妙、很絕，十足是個好方法！」

知名英語教師、廣播主持人
徐薇

「學英文就像談戀愛，沒錯，當你急於與所愛的人溝通、表白自己時，戀愛與英文已走進你的生命中。」

知名文學作家、評論家、主持人
蔡詩萍

名人經驗談

美式思想，東方文化
聶雲是中西最佳典範

主持人/阿雅

　　光是聽聶雲的聲音和看到他的笑容，學習的興致就自然提高了起來。與他合作一年多的時間裡還真學到了不少，不只是他冷不防爆出的一些英文單字，還學到了西方文化看事情的態度。

　　記得有一次我們在廣告空檔時和攝影師們聊天，談起了他們工作的辛苦和繁忙，我在好奇心的驅使之下，忍不住問了攝影師一個月的收入大概多少，只見聶雲哥臉色大變，用著不可思議的眼神看著我說：「My God!你怎麼可以問別人這種問題？太沒禮貌了，OH NO!」我這回才知道，原來在美國人的心裡，關於收入啊、感情啊、工作啊，凡是涉及個人隱私這塊的問題，都不該輕易出口，對他們來說，是很嚴重的冒犯。也還好先有了這個經驗，讓我後來到美國遊學才能毫髮無傷、全身而退！！

　　聶雲哥是中西合併的最佳典範，雖然說他有許多美式思想，比如說：很有紳士風度，一定會Lady's first！(女士優先) 很有國際觀，懂得尊重別人和尊重自己。他也保有了東方的思想，我可以感受到他有一點點的大男人主義 (哈)，還有他會唱很多國台語老歌，唱腔之道地讓我佩服！

　　我想由他這樣一位涉足於東西方文化的人，來為我們解說英語這門學問，是非常適合的。而且英語教學好像一直是聶雲哥身負的使命之一（說之一的原因是，因為他這個人版圖很大，跨足了很多不同的行業，不信下次你們可以問他），出書應該是完成他教英語這個使命的重要里程碑。聰明如他，一定會把他所知道最快、最好、最妙的學習方法通通放進書裡；所以各位看倌們，準備好好享受一場豐富精彩的英文學習旅程吧！！

學習英文，
需要浪漫的情節與美妙的想像力！

說到聶雲，應該說我是先認識他的聲音，才認識他的人。聶雲以前主持ICRT節目，為很多廣告影片配音，他的聲音很棒，發音很正點，英文很流利。我們錄影時有外國朋友，就靠聶雲發揮翻譯功力。

把英文當成戀愛來談，真是個浪漫的點子！我認識的聶雲，本來就很浪漫，不但如此，他的開朗、率真，很容易感染給大家。他是那種毫不做作，想像力豐富，感情很容易表露在臉上的人。我們錄影時，碰到快樂的事或感動的歌，他馬上會掉眼淚，他就是這種真性情的好朋友。

我自己是初中才開始學英文的，我們這代的英文程度卡在中間，出國唸書的就另當別論。說到英文，我也有一段有趣的ABC邂逅：那時，我在加拿大拍電影「候鳥」（女主角是劉若英），拍片空檔，我經常會去附近的公園跑跑步或是練樂器（吉他或薩克斯風）。有一次我帶了薩克斯風到公園練習，那公園我記得叫「Stanley Park」，不久，眼前出現一位妙齡美女，以下是翻譯成中文的對話：

「我想這公園哪來這樣優美的聲音？我一直在找，沒想到竟然在這裡！」

「我是不是吵到別人？」

「沒有，沒有，非常棒！你很厲害，你可以為我演奏一首歌嗎？」

我當然二話不說，演奏那首我的成名曲「你怎麼捨得讓我難過」。她聽完後問我這首那麼好聽的旋律，怎麼她好像沒聽過，歌名是什麼？我當時本來想自豪的說是我的創作，但一時不知道「捨得」該怎麼翻譯，於是我說，喔，沒什麼，只是一首普通的，嗯，世界名曲（哈）！

歌手/黃品源

　　她看起來像學生，長的很漂亮，我那時候還搞不清楚她的背景，正想了解一下時，她卻跟我說：

　　「你怎麼不去大街上演奏，那裡觀光客很多，我光靠這張牌子就賺了不少，你吹幾首好聽的歌，一定可以賺更多。」

　　我才發現，她從背包拿出來的牌子，寫著：「我是外地來的學生，需要錢，請給我零錢吃飯‧‧‧」之類的。

　　那條街上有很多街頭藝術家、也有流浪漢、學生乞丐（加拿大福利很好，學生畢業後很多人不工作，光靠政府補助、不然就在街上乞討。）我想著：這時候如果我請她吃飯，她應該很高興。就在我要採取行動時，突然出現二個衣衫不整的男生，看起來他們好像是同一夥，沒錯，在她的介紹下，他們的確是一起在街上舉牌子賺錢的學生，搞不好其中一個是她的男友。於是，我那才到嘴的話，為了避免誤會，立刻嚥了下去。

　　這段經歷好玩又有趣，也讓我有所體悟：我們這一代英文是屬於「內斂型」的，學了之後一直沒有用，到了國外挖出來用，才發現自己英文也不爛，就是很少用而已。我們為什麼不敢拿出來用？就是因為怕拼湊會出問題，所以不敢講。其實只要有勇氣去聽、去講，愈練，就會愈突飛猛進。我感覺，學英文要有一種「被激發」的潛能，為了談戀愛、或是為了要怎樣，想去用，敢去用，經常用就自然而然會用了。

　　我跟聶雲是海上運動的健將，我們下次要再約去玩風帆，聶雲出書，我祝他書籍大賣，銷量像風帆一樣的狂飆！

說甜言蜜語的英文，
學習語言津津有味！

說到學英文，我屬於五年級生，最初都是聽余光音樂雜誌、聽西洋流行音樂，看流行音樂排行榜billboard music charts、cashbox、聽Air Supply（空中補給合唱團）這樣子練出來。後來進了世新，聽ICRT、聽Wham（渾合唱團），當時ICRT有個主持人叫David Wang（大衛王），很厲害，是台灣人，沒喝過洋墨水，說出道地的英語腔，一口標準流利美語，真是台灣人學英文不是夢的代表！當時他教我記人名如：George Michael 喬治麥可，記成「蟾蜍別哭」（台語發音），或是單字如：dilemma 左右為難、進退兩難之意，記成「地雷馬」，踩地雷就是進不得退不得，發音跟意思馬上就記住了。這些有趣的技巧，都是我學英文的方式，比死背好玩多了。

英文要有興趣，主要得先聽得懂，我記得有一句話非常受用：「語言不是學問，是習慣。」任何的語言，其實離不開環境。台灣使用英文的場合不是很普遍，就算是留學回來的朋友，久而久之不用，語言就會生疏了。語言得「常用」、成為「習慣」、甚至得用語言來「思考」，思考的目的，主要為了讓講出來的話對方能懂。如果不常用語言來思考，一下子會不知道要用什麼樣的字彙來說，這是我學習語言的一些心得。

國中開始，透過ＩＣＲＴ管道開始接觸英文、後來做外景節目，主持「黃金傳奇」啦、「冒險奇兵」，都讓我有機會接觸外國人，也讓我練就了「敢說」的性格。英文這種東西，不講，不知道自己缺什麼。不講，不知道自己的字彙到底記得多少。語言是從單字所構成的，所以，詞彙的充足，就很重要，書到用時方恨少，詞彙愈多，就會更有信心。詞彙每天背10個，算下來一年就可以有3000多個，這樣的累積很可觀，3000多個單字，已經可以演講了。不然一

主持人／曾國城

天記5個，一年也將近2000個，詞彙就像彈藥，彈藥充足，就不怕，接下來就是去用，去説囉！

聶雲説：「學英文就像談戀愛！」這句話太妙了，如果能用英文來談異國戀情，還真不錯哩！談戀愛不光只靠肢體語言，「甜言蜜語」為什麼讓人聽來快樂、舒服，就是因為用説的。我太太是澳洲華裔，嫁給我之後，中文她變好了，英文我變強了，我同化她，她也幫助我，兩人常常一起看雙語發音頻道Discovery Channel（發現之旅頻道）、Animal Planet（動物星球頻道）......或者電影，生活上互相學習、樂趣很多。

聶雲本身在國外長大、求學，後來回台發展，讀者可以感受到：他帶來中西不同的習慣與生活。透過他現身説法，這本書帶來了學英文的樂趣，會引起大家的共鳴，讓大家學起英文來，津津有味！

目錄

目錄

如何使用本書

在本書的鋪陳架構下，你將有所領略，希望讀者會喜歡這本書，本書特色：

聶雲自創的英文戀愛學

自每一章節開始，聶雲將先和您分享他的感情經驗。從小在國外生活、生長的他，如何創造異國情愛經驗，怎樣和外國人「搏感情」，他將透過一套自創的道地英文學習法則，帶你進入愛情英文的花花世界。

史上最道地、最趣味的英文學習書

全書共分五大章節，生動勾勒屬於愛情的精彩過程。從「戀愛篇」、「熱戀篇」、「爭吵篇」、「舊情人篇」和「修成正果篇」，採截每段過程最具代表性的情感事件，撰擬精彩詼諧的幽默對話，揚棄一般語言學習書的單調形式與呆板會話，讓你在捧腹噴飯之餘，將文法及簡單的語彙牢記在心，是本最沒有壓力的趣味英文學習書。

鸚鵡學習法，邊聽邊說，開口錯不了

隨書附贈由聶雲親自錄音之對話學習光碟，讓你邊看邊念邊學，聶雲教你鸚鵡學習法，只要跟著唸、每天跟著唸，包準你會以最自由愉快的方法，快速學會英文！

看圖說英文，好記又容易

本書包括精采圖繪，看圖學英文，馬上身置其境。學英文就要學用得到的英文。生活當中，英文無所不在：酒吧、露天座、客廳、旅館、游泳池……將生活當中會用的英文單字，自然而然的學起來，看圖對照，有趣又好玩！

看圖學英文

戀愛最容易從哪裡開始？酒吧！

1 flamenco dance
2 saxophone
3 whiskey
4 bartender
5 ouzo
6 pizza
7 trombone
8 trumpet
9 cocktail
10 beer
11 waitress
12 tip

CD 01

1 **flamenco dance** 佛朗明歌舞	5 **ouzo** 茴香酒	9 **cocktail** 雞尾酒
2 **saxophone** 薩克斯風	6 **pizza** 披薩	10 **beer** 啤酒
3 **whiskey** 威士忌	7 **trombone** 伸縮喇叭	11 **waitress** 女服務生
4 **bartender** 酒保	8 **trumpet** 小喇叭	12 **tip** 小費

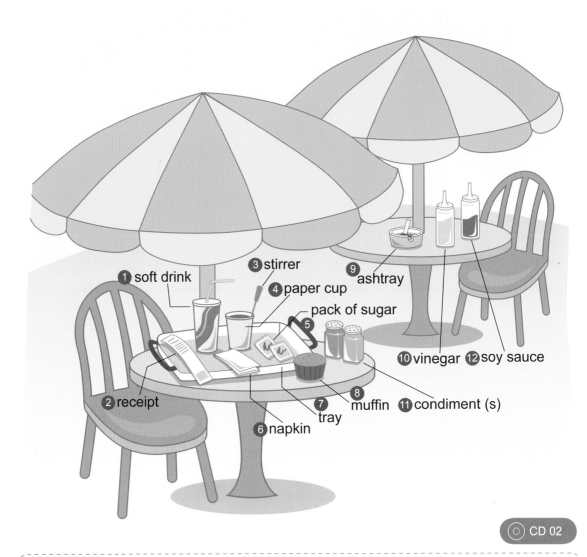

看圖學英文

戀愛最容易從哪裡開始？ 露天座！

- ① soft drink
- ③ stirrer
- ④ paper cup
- ⑨ ashtray
- pack of sugar
- ⑤
- ⑩ vinegar ⑫ soy sauce
- ② receipt
- ⑧
- ⑦ tray
- muffin ⑪ condiment (s)
- ⑥ napkin

◎ CD 02

① **soft drink** 不含酒精的飲料	⑤ **pack of sugar** 糖包	⑨ **ashtray** 煙灰缸
② **receipt** 收據	⑥ **napkin** 紙巾	⑩ **vinegar** 醋
③ **stirrer** 攪拌棒	⑦ **tray** 托盤	⑪ **condiment (s)** 調味料
④ **paper cup** 紙杯	⑧ **muffin** 鬆糕	⑫ **soy sauce** 醬油

看圖學英文

熱戀從情侶一起去旅行開始？旅館大廳。

- ① clerk
- ② pamphlet
- ③ reception desk
- ④ guest
- ⑤ tour guide
- ⑥ luggage
- ⑦ newspaper rack
- ⑧ luggage cart
- ⑨ doorman
- ⑩ lobby
- ⑪ escalator
- ⑫ bellhop
- elecator

① clerk 職員	⑤ tour guide 旅遊指南	⑨ doorman 門房
② pamphlet 小手冊	⑥ luggage 行李	⑩ lobby 大廳
③ reception desk 接待處	⑦ newspaper rack 書報架	⑪ escalator 手扶梯
④ guest 客人	⑧ luggage cart 行李推車	⑫ bellhop 行李服務生

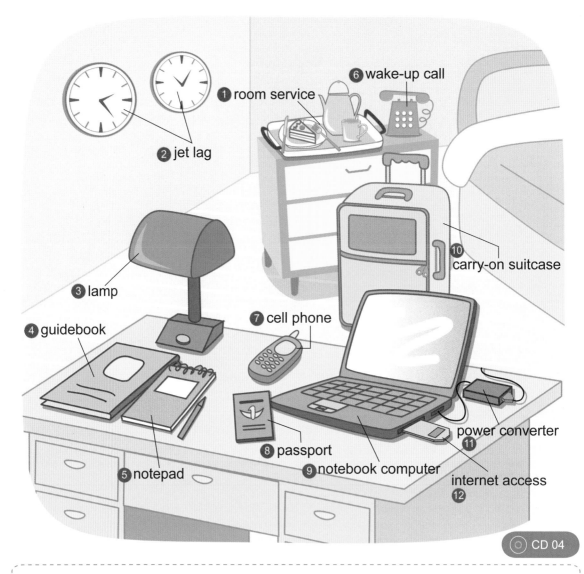

看圖學英文

熱戀從哪裡最容易發酵？ 旅館內。

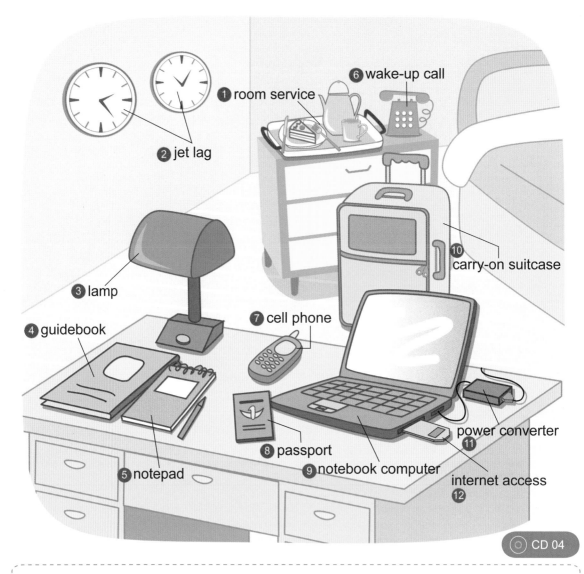

① room service
② jet lag
⑥ wake-up call
③ lamp
④ guidebook
⑦ cell phone
⑩ carry-on suitcase
⑧ passport
⑨ notebook computer
⑤ notepad
⑪ power converter
⑫ internet access

CD 04

① room service 客房送餐服務　⑤ notepad 便條本　⑨ notebook computer 筆記型電腦

② jet lag 時差　⑥ wake-up call 叫醒服務　⑩ carry-on suitcase 手提行李

③ lamp 檯燈　⑦ cell phone 手機　⑪ power converter 變壓器

④ guidebook 導覽手冊　⑧ passport 護照　⑫ internet access 網路連結

爭吵的時候，你是你，我是我？

CD 05

① stretch 伸展運動	⑤ swimming cap 泳帽	⑨ life preserver 救生圈
② dumbbell 啞鈴	⑥ bikini 比基尼	⑩ treadmill 跑步機
③ barbell 槓鈴	⑦ lounge chair 躺椅	⑪ coach 教練
④ jump rope 跳繩	⑧ goggles 泳鏡	⑫ scale 體重計

爭吵之後，竟不經意想起舊情人的東西？

1 music box
11 mug
4 jewelry box
9 teddy bear
5 necklace
6 anklet
2 chain
7 pendant
12 cat litter
8 bracelet
10 litter box
3 picture frame

CD 06

1 music box 音樂盒	5 necklace 項鍊	9 teddy bear 泰迪熊
2 chain 鍊子	6 anklet 腳鍊	10 litter box 砂盆
3 picture frame 相框	7 pendant 墜子	11 mug 馬克杯
4 jewelry box 珠寶盒	8 bracelet 手鐲	12 cat litter 貓砂

戀愛修成正果，美麗家庭就在眼前！

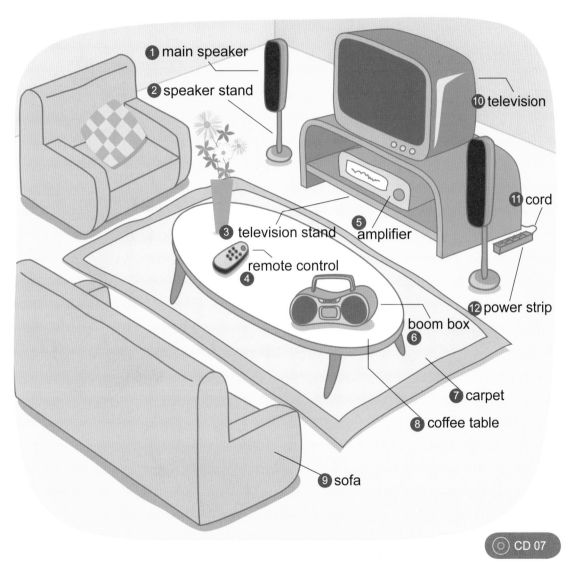

1. **main speaker** 主喇叭
2. **speaker stand** 喇叭架
3. **television stand** 電視架
4. **remote control** 遙控器
5. **amplifier** 擴大機
6. **boom box** 手提音響
7. **carpet** 地毯
8. **coffee table** 茶几
9. **sofa** 沙發
10. **television** 電視機
11. **cord** 電線
12. **power strip** 排插座

戀愛修成正果時，也是歡樂開始時！

① haunted house
③ Ferris wheel
④ carousel
② ticket booth
⑤ food stand
⑪ gift shop
⑨ hot dog
⑥ camera
⑩ popcorn
⑦ tripod
⑫ roller coaster
⑧ clown

CD 08

① **haunted house** 鬼屋	⑤ **food stand** 小吃攤	⑨ **hot dog** 熱狗
② **ticket booth** 售票亭	⑥ **camera** 照相機	⑩ **popcorn** 爆米花
③ **Ferris wheel** 摩天輪	⑦ **tripod** 三腳架	⑪ **gift shop** 禮品店
④ **carousel** 旋轉木馬	⑧ **clown** 小丑	⑫ **roller coaster** 雲霄飛車

5招讓你英文突飛猛進

- ## 大量閱讀,尤其閱讀英文相關書報刊物、甚至廣告DM

  我建議大家多多閱讀報紙、雜誌、廣告,這樣可以吸收各類資訊,讓自己的視野拓寬。從中文閱讀到英文閱讀,不要害怕,一步一步跨出去,我記得很多從台灣去美國念書的朋友,總是搜集英文報紙、英文雜誌,東看西看、東問西問,連英文廣告DM都不放過,就是因為廣告上有很多實用的生活語法,比如:**buy one get one free**(買一送一),這類跟生活結合的英文,一看就懂,好記又實用。

- ## 上網、看電視、聽廣播

  現在科技發達,上網是學英文的好方法。多看一些自己有興趣的英文網站,可以增加學習興趣。此外,看電視**CNN**、聽廣播**ICRT**,都是增強聽力的方式。但是大家不要只是看、只是聽,要學會去analyze(分析).....真正了解事件或主題的涵意。怎麼樣測試自己有沒有完全了解呢?我建議大家用錄音機錄下一小段,等過幾天後,放出來聽聽,如果你還記得事件內容,就表示這些英文已經深入你心中了。

- ## 加強各領域的專業知識,比如:經濟、政治、法律、科學...等

  如果想要真正成為一個英文通,那一定要針對各領域有些程度與了解,平常就要多知道經濟、政治、法律、科學等相關知識。這樣即使有不了解的英文,一旦與自己熟知的專業領域對起來,很容易就了解並融會貫通。比如Economic depression這個字,Economic是「經濟上的」意思,depression是「沮喪」的意思,如果有經濟學背景,很快就可以了解是「經濟蕭條」,而不會搞不清楚狀況。

- ## 出國旅遊

  出國旅遊絕對是增進英文能力的好方法。住在一個英語系國家一段時間,老實說,英文不熟也要熟了,每天醒來聽到的語言就是英文,逃都逃不掉。如果不能長期待在英語系國家生活,建議大家不妨分階段,每年計畫一次旅行,每次十幾天,每次待在同一個地方,感覺當地的生活,與當地人做朋友。

- ## 讓英文變成自己永遠的追求者

  學英文哇哇叫苦,一定是方法不對!學英文就好像談戀愛一樣,一直會想去探究,永遠有無止盡的好奇與熱情。我建議大家要把英文變成自己永遠的追求者,學習永無止境,語言也一樣,只會愈學愈多,愈學愈好。

把英文當情人

因為工作，我常常往返世界各地，尤其經常在台灣和大陸飛來飛去。不管到哪，英文總是一個很好用的工具，英文就像一把鑰匙，帶我通往全世界。因為具備了這樣的語言能力，不管在主持台灣、香港或新馬等亞洲的跨國性節目，或者國際性的優質節目如 Discovery Channel（發現之旅頻道）邀我推薦台灣旅遊景點......「英文」，經常是我勝出成為主持最佳人選的因素之一。我想，在無國界的社會中，英文，是必備的基本能力。

我一直想寫一本英文學習書，但是這麼多年來，超過不下數十家的出版社找過我，希望出一本語言學習書，我都加以婉拒，為什麼？

我發現不管是台灣或大陸，年輕學子為了通過英文考試，補習、啃教科書...坊間的語言學習書TOEFL（托福）、TOEIC、GRE、GMAT、GEPT（全民英檢）多不勝數，學習英語，成了學生恐怖的經驗。

對我來說，「學習，應該是一件愉快的事！」「學英文，更是一件有趣而毫不費力的事情！」所以，當時報數位出版營運長Karen和編輯主任May來找我洽談出書事宜，基於同樣理念，我們都希望朝這樣的方向努力，於是出版了我的第一本語言學習書。

我想出版怎樣的英語學習書呢？我想出一本趣味、生活實用、由淺入深、神靈活現、好讀好玩、輕鬆有趣的英語學習書。簡而言之，我想出一本和戀愛有關的英文書，我會這樣說，是因為我知道只有把英文當成情人，你才會真正擁有學習的樂趣！

有位中英雙語教授（Bilingual professor）跟我說過，當你在夢中講話時連對白都出現英文，那表示你可以真正學好英文。這位教授與我的想法很接近，當你把英文當作情人，朝思暮想，學習英文就像追逐愛情的過程，當你進入到這樣的學習情境，英語學習，就不是苦藥，而是一種興趣、喜好。這就是我想要帶給大家的一種學習感受，一種不為了考試、升學、應付的投機學習，一種真正發自內心喜愛，有興趣、逐步成長、優質的累積學習。

《戀愛英文ABC》就是這樣一本好玩有趣的英文學習書。你會發現，這本書所有的會話，都是當今時下年輕人常用的英文。語言是活的，在美國每天都不斷有新的用語出現，我想教大家的，就是這些很實用、很鮮活的口語表達。讀完本書，你會真的發現，學英文的四大方向：聽、說、讀、寫，跟談戀愛一樣：

溝通妙法，「聽」情人「說」話

溝通方式很多，「聽」和「說」是最直接的一種，在聽與說的過程中，情人的習慣和個性會顯露，很直接，只要你在相處的過程中夠用心專注，多聽多溝通，就不會引起許多誤會。

「讀」懂文法，就像理解情人的生活習慣

瞭解英文文法，就像理解情人的生活習慣。你只有去看去讀，細心了解情人的生活習慣，才能逐漸贏得情人的心！

「寫」出情人感動的情書

承諾不必說，能寫出一封文情並茂的情書，可立即為戀愛加分不少。

大家有沒有發現，學英文真的跟談戀愛一樣，先充分理解「情人性格＝文法」，透過戀愛中的「情人溝通＝聽＋說」，然後順利地將愛意訴諸文字「感動情人＝寫」，聽＋說＋讀＋寫＝學好英文！大家覺得學英文好不好玩呢？追求愛情的過程，酸、甜、苦、辣都有，學習英文也一樣，但是一旦修成正果，英文到手之後，你就海闊天空自由翔翔了！現在，就讓我們用追求愛情的態度，進入英文好玩的學習吧！

怎樣學英文最**快**

　　我的周圍，有許多朋友想學好英文，但是許多朋友學的很痛苦。我想，怎麼會呢？我回想小時候學英文的經驗，我七歲時移民美國，當時年紀雖小，但已經可以感覺到異國的隔閡。剛去美國時，我也有患得患失的心情，不曉得如何和不同膚色、不同語言的小朋友打交道。後來實在太想跟隔壁的金髮美眉講話了，於是很自然就開口說英語。所以當有朋友問我：「怎樣學英文最快？」我會回答：「談戀愛最快。」《戀愛英文ABC》就是一本以戀愛過程為基調的英文學習書，我的出發點，就是想幫助大家破解學習英文之苦。說到這，有幾個觀念不能不先跟大家心理建設一下：

學英文就像談戀愛，第一件重要的事情是－－「要放膽！」

追女孩要大膽，學英文也一樣，需要大膽說出來，不要懷疑，就是像嬰兒牙牙學語一樣，從嗯嗯啊啊、胡言亂語中，抓住發音的技巧。說到這裡，感覺跟戀愛很像，不是嗎？從初識到相愛，從熱戀到分開，從感動到感慨，從狂喜到悲哀，學英文真的跟戀愛一樣，五味雜陳，只有戀愛過、勇敢身歷其中的人才知道。

學英文就像談戀愛，第二件重要的事情是－－「Nothing to lose」(沒有什麼好損失的)

女孩就算沒把到，總也學到失敗的教訓，記取了教訓與經驗，下一次會更好。學英文這件事也一樣，只要你努力過，就會累積點什麼經驗，比如單字，每天記一個，一個月至少也記二十來個，長久下來，字彙量不可小覷。

學英文就像談戀愛，第三件重要的事情是－－「學像樣的英文」

好像台灣人看到老外就認為他英文很棒，其實不盡然喔，美國也有文盲，或許有人不相信，美國那麼發達，怎麼還會有文盲？實際上美國文盲還真不少。根據資料顯示，美國至少有2千6百萬人是文盲或半文盲，成人中有22%不會讀書看報，有16%不會寫字，在聯合國159個會員國中，美國人的識字率排名第49位。大家想想，一個文盲或半文盲的人來教英文，這就好像，怎麼說，好像一個老外交中文，或是一個流氓教小孩說話，說出來話總是有點不像樣的感覺。所以我說，學英文就像談戀愛，至少戀愛中男女用的英文，總不會不潔與不雅吧！

我談的那場戀愛．．．

　　我一直覺得人們對異性的好奇，是種很奇妙的經驗。可能在某個年歲，某一瞬間之後，我們對異性的嚮往便開始源源不絕。

　　那一刻就發生在我第一眼看到Julie的時候，那時我十四歲。那時候，我已經在美國生活了幾年。我到現在都還記得她的容貌與身影，她是很典型的金髮女孩，圓圓的臉蛋，有著一對發亮的藍眼睛。她優雅的穿著打扮，好像童話故事中的小公主。當她走進我的視線，我有種手足失措，快要痙攣的感覺，一直到今天，我都還清楚的記得。

　　每年的情人節，學校都會安排一些活動，其中一個活動在情人節的前兩週舉行，那天到來的時候，老師們會在學校操場上，擺上一張桌子，接受同學訂花。我還記得那時只能送康乃馨，一朵五毛錢。為了送花，我整整四天沒有喝牛奶，最後攢了兩朵下來。好吧！我承認自己有點「卒仔」，那回我沒敢署名，只在包裝花的塑膠封套上，註記了「secret admirer」（秘密的仰慕者）

　　情人節當天的第二堂課，也就是花要送到的時刻，我還記得當那堂課結束之後，我利用短短的休息時間，在人海中找尋我的金髮女孩。當我看到她手上拿著不止兩朵的康乃馨（有紅色及粉紅色…），臉上有著公主似的驕傲與得意。我感到安心，當然，也「皮皮挫」：有對手相爭！

　　學校辦了一個情人節舞會，這是我生平第一次參加舞會，當我在偌大的舞池找到Julie時，已接近舞會尾聲，我揣想著：如果我沒在這首慢歌結束之前約到她，今天的舞會大概就沒有希望了！於是，我鼓足勇氣，悄悄靠近女孩。Julie像是人群中唯一的發光體，那時，我只能看見她。我向她吞吞吐吐地說了：「Julie, would you like to dance？」（Julie, 想跳舞嗎？）她看見我，神情

有些訝異，愣了一會，簡單地一句「sure」(好啊！)，我們於是緩緩步入舞池。

她把手掛在我的脖子上，我右手扶著她的腰，那是我生平的第一支舞，但我們兩人之間的距離大概可以......嗯，再站兩個人吧！（哈）

「Would you like to go around with me？」是當時美國孩子間流傳的用法，用來吊馬子，以輕鬆的態度，問對方「要不要跟我在一起？」。我如法炮製，就問這句，嘿嘿，我們成了一對。這該算是我的初戀吧！（笑）

 浪漫小語

Would you like to go around with me?

這是美國年青人把妹經常流傳的用法，用一種輕鬆的態度，試探性地問對方「要不要跟我在一起？」學起這句話還算好用，不會因為太嚴肅而嚇跑美眉。

愛情實戰
Love at first sight
一見鍾情

 CD 09

Dennis: Do you believe in love at first sight?

May: How can you believe in love at first sight in a city which guys can pee in the MRT station?

Dennis: I see. I think love at first sight only happens between superstars and models. The women in the city would check your credit record and physical evaluation before going out with you.

May: Yup. But I truly think the best way to convince nonbelievers is for them to experience the magic feeling of love at first sight.

譯 對話譯點通

Dennis: 你相信一見鍾情嗎？

May: 在一個連地鐵站都能看見有人小便的城市裡，你怎能相信一見鍾情？

Dennis: 我了解。一見鍾情這檔事只發生在巨星和名模之間，這城市裡，女人和你交往之前，得先看過你的信用卡資料和體檢表。

May: 對啊，但是我認為要說服那些不信的人，最好的方法就是：讓他們去體驗一見鍾情的神奇感覺。

字 單字及片語

love at first sight	n.一見鍾情
sight	n.視線
MRT station	n.地鐵站
pee	v.小號
credit	n.信用
record	n.紀錄
credit record	n.信用資料
evaluation	n.評估
physical evaluation	n.體檢表
yup	v. 是的，yes的俏皮說法，也可以說 yeah，比較嬉皮的味道

老美在說yes的時候，經常會有一些小小的變化，yup (或作yep) 和yeah同樣都是yes的意思。yup聽來簡捷有力，給人非常確定、肯定的感覺。比如：**Do you want to go? Yup.** (你要去嗎？是的。) yeah 聽起來比較鬆散，同樣同意對方看法，但是態度很輕鬆，不嚴肅。比如：**That movie was so funny. Yeah, I guess so.** (那電影有夠好笑。是啊，我想是吧！)

愛情實戰
chat up
搭訕

 CD 10

(In a piano bar, a 70-year-old man meets a pretty woman)

Dennis: Excuse me, have we met somewhere before?

Eileen: No, I am afraid not.

Dennis: Well, can I buy you a drink?

Eileen: I already have one, thanks.

Dennis: May I buy you an island?

Eileen: I don't know, can you?

Dennis: My name is Dennis.

Eileen: Eileen.

Dennis: So Eileen, do you come here often?

Eileen: Honey, the frequency is older than you are.

對話譯點通

（鋼琴酒吧裡，一位70高齡的男人邂逅一位妙齡女郎）

Dennis: 不好意思，我們以前見過嗎？

Eileen: 恐怕沒有吧！

Dennis: 好吧！那我可以請你一杯飲料嗎？

Eileen: 我已經有一杯了，謝了！

Dennis: 那我可以買座島給妳嗎？

Eileen: 我不知道，你可以嗎？

Dennis: 我的名字叫Dennis。

Eileen: 我叫Eileen。

Dennis: 你常來這裡嗎？Eileen？

Eileen: 親愛的，我來這的次數比你的年紀還大呢！！

 單字及片語

chat up	v.搭訕	搭訕的其他講法（有打開話匣子之意） hit on somebody strike up a conversation start a conversation break the ice
excuse me	不好意思，經常用於借過，或要打斷什麼事情。	
be afraid (of)+N	害怕什麼	
afraid not	恐怕沒有	
frequency	n. 經常性、表示頻繁	

搭訕番外篇
Dennis心法傳授
pub看風水

　　在日常生活裡，我不是一個迷信風水的人，但是在pub裡，那可就不一樣了。你所處的位子，絕對與你接下來的優勝劣敗有吉凶關係。是的，好位子可以展現你的份量，好像一個黃金店面，人潮源源不絕，這也就等於說，你搭訕的機會變多了。讓我們言歸正傳，就我多年的經驗，pub的最佳風水就在吧台靠近啤酒的出口處，Bartender因為工作所需，總會在此多做停留，所以不妨在此多加逗留，一旦機會來臨，你就能夠瀟灑的、快速的取走酒保手中啤酒，而不是很遜卡的捻著零錢，在那裡苦苦排隊卻等不到一杯飲料。

　　如果是包廂式環境，絕對要找角落窩，角落的位子永遠勝過中間的開闊，為什麼？因為「角落」是親密關係最佳的醞釀場所。當你和心儀對象搭訕時，角落的居處將縮小你們之間的距離，親密感覺自然發生。倘若你就坐在轉角的沙發椅上，雙手搭靠椅背，兩腿交岔，那瀟灑的氣勢，馬上讓人感覺歡迎來「love corner」(愛的小窩)之勢，效果當然不同凡響。

　　最後，有個位子請你千萬別低估它的實用性，雖然聽起來有點煞風景，但是以其天然地利之便，此處絕對稱得上是個「龍位」，那個位子就是廁所前方。怎麼說呢？因為那裡音樂聲通常不太大，當尿遁的人增加，排隊如廁的隊伍加長，便能給你更多的時空條件運籌帷幄，就算是發現苗頭不對，也可直奔廁所，獲得掩護，這裡絕對可以秉持我們「進可攻、退可守」的搭訕最高指導原則。

愛情實戰
have a date
約會

 CD 11

Amy: I have a date with Michael tonight.

Dennis: Who's the lucky guy?

Amy: Well, we met in the supermarket around the corner and we both love the chef's salad.

Dennis: hmmmm, you're going out with him because you like the same salad. I'd look into it some more if I were you.

Amy: What'd you mean?

Dennis: Before going out with the guy, check his credit record and physical evaluation. That's all I'm saying. There are too many weirdoes out there.

Amy: Yup, and you're one of them.

對話譯點通

Amy: 我今晚和**Michael**有個約會。

Dennis: 是嗎？！那幸運的傢伙是誰？

Amy: 我們在轉角口的那間超市遇到，而且我們不約而同都愛吃主廚沙拉！

Dennis: 嗯**...**你們要一起出去的原因，只是因為都同樣喜歡吃主廚沙拉。如果我是你，我會再多深入了解一些。

Amy: 你的意思是？

Dennis: 在和他那傢伙出去之前，先確認他的信用資料和體檢表，那就是我想説的，外面有太多怪卡了！

Amy: 沒錯，你就是其中之一。

 單字及片語

have a date	約會
supermarket	n.超級市場
around the corner	在轉角口
chef salad	n.主廚沙拉
look into	v.看深入些
If I were you	假如我是你，這裡是假設語氣，所以用過去式were
What'd you mean?	你是什麼意思？
weirdo (es)	n.怪卡，複數+es

愛情實戰
First impression
第一印象

 CD 12

Dennis 小提醒：
老美會用blind date（盲目的約會）來形容素未謀面
的朋友聚會。

(in a restaurant, a matchmaker introduces a foreign guy to a Taiwanese woman and let's see what happens then...)

Woman: This restaurant is famous for their steamed pork and it tastes great, doesn't it?

Man: I'm new to the restaurant so anything that is good enough for you is good enough for me. (murmuring) For someone your size you must know your food and plus, you might be able to bench more than I can so I won't argue with you there.

Woman: You won't be sorry! (murmuring) The way he eats it's as if he hasn't eaten for days, but look at him, he's all bones. What is he, anorexic? Or has not he heard of a gym before?

Man: Well, I'm glad we are on this date. You are the beautiful and athletic type that every man longs for.

Woman: You're too kind. You have that perfect, lean and cut body that only super models have.

譯 對話譯點通

（餐廳裡，媒人想撮合一對異國男女，讓我們來看看接下來會發生什麼？）

女人：這間餐廳以這道燉豬肉聞名，它真的很好吃，不是嗎？

男人：我是第一次來這家餐廳，不是那麼熟這裡的美食，所以任何你覺得好吃的食物，我也覺得好吃。（喃喃自語）對於你這樣大尺寸的人來說，你一定很懂得美食，而且，你甚至有可能舉重贏過我哩，所以在這方面我還是別跟你爭論。

女人：你不會後悔的。（喃喃自語）這傢伙吃東西的樣子簡直像幾天沒吃過東西一樣！看看他，全身都是皮包骨，發生啥事啦？得厭食症嗎？他有聽過健身房嗎？

男人：嗯，我真的很高興我們有這次的約會，你是屬於漂亮、運動家的類型，每個男人都很心儀渴望喔！

女人：你太客氣了，你那完美、纖瘦、肌塊緊實的身材，看來只有超級男模才有呢。

字 單字及片語

matchmaker	n.媒人
be famous for	以...聞名
steamed pork	n.燉豬肉
new to the restaurant	第一次來這家餐廳
Anything that is good enough for you is good enough for me.	任何事，你好我就好
bench	v.舉重
argue with someone	與某人爭論
murmur	v.喃喃自語、碎碎念
anorexic	n. 厭食症
gym	n.健身房 gymnasium的縮寫
athletic type	n .運動家的體型，表示體格健壯
long for	v. 渴望追求、心儀
lean	adj.瘦的
cut body	結實的肌肉和身材，cut在這裡是形容詞，雕塑的意思。

愛情實戰

excuse

藉口

(a couple in a Chinese restaurant)

Kelly: Where were you last night?

Dennis: I was working in the office.

Kelly: Can you get the dinner bill?

Dennis: I forgot my wallet.

Kelly: I've fallen out of love.

Dennis: That's because we are married.

Kelly: That is your excuse.

對話譯點通

（一對夫妻在一家中國飯館）

Kelly: 你昨晚在哪？

Dennis: 我在公司工作。

Kelly: 你可以付今天的晚餐錢嗎？

Dennis: 我忘記帶我的皮夾啦！

Kelly: 我們的感情越來越淡了。

Dennis: 那是因為我們已經結婚了！

Kelly: 那是你的藉口。

 單字及片語

excuse	n.藉口
couple	n. 情侶、夫妻
to get the dinner bill	v. 付晚餐費用
wallet	n. 皮夾
fall out of love	v. 感情用罄
are married	結婚了

愛情實戰
pub
夜店

CD 14

(in a pub, a man meets a woman)

Dennis: That's a pretty outfit.

Amy: Thanks!

Dennis: Haven't I seen you here before?

Amy: I am afraid not. This is my first time here.

Dennis: My name is Dennis.

Amy: Amy.

Dennis: So, Amy! Would you like to dance?

Amy: I am sorry, it's too late and I have to go.

Dennis: Me too. Could I give you a lift?

Amy: You never quit, do you?

Dennis: Well, that depends on who I meet!

對話譯點通

（夜店裡，一名男子邂逅一名女子）

Dennis: 妳穿得真美！

Amy: 謝了！

Dennis: 我以前好像在這裡看過妳？

Amy: 恐怕沒有喔！這次我第一次到這！

Dennis: 我叫做**Dennis**。

Amy: 我是**Amy**！

Dennis: 嗯，**Amy**！要不要一起跳舞？！

Amy: 抱歉！有點晚了，我得走了！

Dennis: 我也是，那我可以載妳一程嗎？

Amy: 你不會放棄的，是嗎？

Dennis: 那得看我遇見的是誰了！

 單字及片語

outfit	n.外衣、裝束
Would you like to dance?	願意跳舞嗎？

類似的邀舞說法還有...
Care to dance?
You want to dance?
Could I have the next dance?
May I have the next dance?

Could I give you a lift?	我可以載你一程嗎？

類似的用法還有......
Need a lift?
Need a ride?
（需要搭便車嗎？）

quit	v.放棄、戒除
ex: He decided to quit smoking.	例：（他決定戒煙了。）

that depends +OOO	得看OOO情況
to depend on/upon	依靠OOO人或事物
=be dependent on/upon	

愛情實戰

harassment

騷擾

CD 15

Dennis: Hi, What's your name?

Cathy: I'm sorry, do I know you?

Dennis: I'm Dennis... Now you do.

Cathy: Oh, well I'm here with some friends so I have to get back now.

Dennis: Why don't you stay and talk to me for a while?

Cathy: I said I need to go. Please leave me alone.

Dennis: Oh, come on. There's no need to be mean.

Cathy: Don't touch me or I will call the cops.

Dennis: Ok Ok!

譯 對話譯點通

Dennis: Hi！請問妳怎麼稱呼？

Cathy: 不好意思，我不認識你！

Dennis: 我是Dennis，那你現在認識啦！

Cathy: 喔！我跟我朋友一起來，我得走了！

Dennis: 妳怎麼不多坐坐和我說說話？

Cathy: 我說了，我要走了，離我遠點。

Dennis: 喔～不要這樣嘛，沒有必要那麼兇嘛！

Cathy: 不要碰我喔！否則我要叫警察了！

Dennis: 好吧好吧！

 字 單字及片語

harassment	n.騷擾
for a while	一下子
leave me alone	讓我靜一靜
come on	別這樣嘛
mean	a.粗魯、兇
cops	n.警察，這是日常生活口語化稱呼警察的用法。

愛情實戰
dating foreigners
與外國人交往

 CD 16

> Dennis 小提醒：
> 前頭我們提到，「Date」有約會的意思，於是，
> 「Dating foreigners」就是和外國人談戀愛的
> 意思。

Linda: Hey, Dennis, I'd like to tell you something.

Dennis: What's that?

Linda: Well, I met a cute guy at the night club yesterday and he is a foreigner.

Dennis: Is this your first time to go on a date with a non-Taiwanese guy?

Linda: Yeah, do you have any advice?

Dennis: First of all, you should know that foreign guys tend to be more forward and aggressive than Taiwanese guys. But remember there are plenty of creeps out there, and it makes no difference where they're from.

Linda: Well, I hope this love experience will have a happy ending.

譯 對話譯點通

Linda: 嘿，Dennis，我想跟你説件事！

Dennis: 説啥？

Linda: 就是啊...我昨晚在夜店碰到一個可愛的帥哥，而他是個外國人。

Dennis: 這是妳第一次和非台灣人以外的男人拍拖嗎？

Linda: 是啊！你有什麼建議嗎？

Dennis: 首先，你要知道，外國人比台灣人要直接、積極多了，而且要謹記，不管外國人還是台灣人，都有很多討厭鬼。

Linda: 是嗎？總之我希望這段感情能有個好結果！

字 單字及片語

foreigner	n. 外國人
Hey	嗨，打招呼語，跟Hi同樣意思。
non-Taiwanese	非台灣人
First of all	首先（常作為語句的開場白）
tend to	v. 傾向於...
forward	adj. 直接的
aggressive	adj. 企圖心強的、積極的
active	adj. 積極的
plenty of	很多，後面要加名詞複數
creep	n. 討厭鬼，複數加s
happy ending	美好的結局

愛情實戰
material girl
拜金女

 CD 17

> **Dennis** 小提醒：
> 「**material girl**」是瑪丹娜多年前的暢銷歌曲，
> 是指「拜物」、以物質為上的女孩。最近有個時興
> 的同義字叫「**gold digger**」(淘金者)和我們形容
> 的拜金女頗有異曲同工之妙，讀者不妨學起來唷！

Dennis: Hey, Rose. Do you know that blonde girl living in your neighborhood?

Rose: Which one, the pretty one?

Dennis: Yeah, the hot one.

Rose: Oh, that's Helen. Yes, she's my neighbor.

Dennis: You have to introduce me!

Rose: Come on! Haven't you heard about that girl? I suggest you to keep away from her.

Dennis: What's wrong with her?

Rose: Well, she is notorious for being a material girl and wants nothing but money from you. Before going out with you, she will check to see if you are able to afford all her needs.

Dennis: That's terrible, thanks for telling me. So when can you hook me up?

Rose: What? Did you hear a word I said? She uses her men, takes their money, and dumps them after they run out of cash.

Dennis: With a body like that? She can use me anytime she wants.

Rose: Men are such suckers!

對話譯點通

Dennis: 嘿，Rose，妳認識那個住在妳家附近的那個金髮女孩嗎？

Rose: 哪一個？很漂亮的那個嗎？

Dennis: 對，就是那個很辣的女孩！

Rose: 喔，那是Helen，是啊！她是我的鄰居！

Dennis: 妳一定要幫我介紹一下。

Rose: 拜託，你沒聽説過那個女生的事嗎？我勸你還是離她遠一點！

Dennis: 那個女孩怎麼了？

Rose: 她是一個惡名昭彰的拜金女，啥都不要，就是要你的錢！和你出去約會之前，她會知道你能不能負擔她所有的需要。

Dennis: 那真恐怖！謝謝你告訴我，那你什麼時候要介紹給我？

Rose: 什麼？你聽到我説的嗎？她利用男友，花他們的錢，發現對方沒錢了就甩了他們。

Dennis: 有那樣的身材，只要她願意，她任何時間都可以利用我。

Rose: 男人真是笨蛋！

單字及片語

material girl	n.拜金女
hot	adj. 熱的。形容女生很辣！
you have to introduce me	你一定要幫我介紹
keep away from	離某人遠一點
notorious	a. 惡名昭彰的
afford	v. 負擔
terrible	adj. 恐怖的
thanks for	為...謝謝，後面動詞要加ing
dump	v.拋棄
sucker	n笨蛋

還可以説：
Hook me up

愛情實戰
rich and powerful family
豪門

 CD 18

Dennis 小提醒：
除了上述的說法，豪門也可寫為「**wealthy and influential clan**」。**Clan** 意指「家族」、「集團」。

Kelly: Getting married with a man from a rich and powerful family is many girls' dreams.

Dennis: Yeah! But I've heard plenty of stories and it is tough to maintain a relationship like that. Some say that a guy with time and cash is a combination for trouble. I think you are much better off with a poor solid guy like me!

Kelly: Poor? Yes. But solid? I don't think so. I think you're just jealous.

對話譯點通

Kelly: 嫁入豪門是許多女孩的夢想。

Dennis: 是啊！但是我聽了許多關於豪門的故事，要維繫豪門的婚姻關係並不容易。有人説男人只要有閒有錢，就會惹事生非。我想，跟我這樣一個沒錢、踏實務實的人絕對好多了。

Kelly: 沒錢？同意，踏實務實？不必了吧！你只是在忌妒而已。

單字及片語

getting married with	與(人)結婚
tough	adj. 棘手的、費勁的、有難度的
maintain	v. 維繫
combination	n.結合
a poor solid guy	窮而踏實的人
jealous	adj. 忌妒

熱戀

我談的那場戀愛...

　　熱戀，是一段戀情最甜蜜的時光，當你陷入熱戀期，會極度在意情人，好像這世上的所有事情都不重要（哈）。熱戀時的想念，是一種無時無刻、無所不在的神奇經驗，我和一般人一樣，也擁有過這種不可言喻的時刻。

　　這段經驗發生在和Judy相識的時候。為了把握難得的假日，我特地安排了一次旅行，一方面想和Judy共同編織一次浪漫的旅行，另一方面也為了和朋友炫耀（哈，虛榮心作祟啦），我們展開了一趟公路旅行（Road Trip）。

　　從美國西岸的洛杉磯出發，一直到舊金山，這段旅程，只有我和Judy共享。那天，天氣很好，陽光很亮、天空很藍，微風徐徐，沿途中，我們哼哼唱唱，渾然不覺旅途的辛勞。

　　我們的第一站是加州中部最大的一座農場（Bakersfield），我知道Judy喜歡吃水果，就選擇這世外桃源，算是送給她的第一份禮物。農場裡的空氣飄著果香：桃子、葡萄、柳橙、檸檬…酸酸甜甜的，像我們沈醉熱戀的感覺，Judy笑著說她這輩子從沒見過這麼多的水果同時在一起，我們就這樣一山吃過一山。我們好像童話故事裡，走進糖果屋的孩子，笑著、訝異著，等不及將水果洗盡，連皮帶肉的吞進嘴裡，幸福和滿足，都寫在臉上。

　　傍晚，我們抵達Napa Valley， Napa Valley以葡萄酒、葡萄產量而聞名，至今仍維持著相當溫馨的小鎮風情，整座城，除了主街上商店林立之外，放眼望去，都是葡萄園。住在裡面，有遺世獨立的感覺。那裡的人彼此熟悉、夜不閉戶，酒場主人對遠道而來的我們，極盡熱情款待，介紹客人品嚐珍貴的葡萄酒，甚至慷慨相送，我和Judy沿路品嚐新釀的美酒，快樂極了。如果說這裡是南加州最浪漫的地方，我舉雙手贊成。

　　我和Judy就這樣帶著地圖完成這趟公路旅行，隨性所至，想到哪就到哪，當時的我們，正處於熱戀狀態，所到之處，心中都是美景佳人。"Everything looks perfect！"（每件事情都完美），看到她的笑容，讓我感覺，連飛翔的海鷗、路邊的花，都在微笑！"Love me a little less, but love me longer。"（愛我少一點，但愛我久一點。），我當下非常渴望與Judy長廂廝守，那是我第一次動了結婚的念頭。

 浪漫小語

Love me a little less, but love me longer.

「愛我少一點，但愛我久一點。」熱戀中的情人，怕對方愛的時間短了些，寧願對方愛少一點，所以就有了這句話。

愛情實戰
pick up
把上、釣（馬子／凱子）

 CD 19

(Carrie and his female friend, Eileen are having lunch in a restaurant. In the meantime, a waitress sends them a bottle of red wine)

Eileen: We didn't order red wine.

Waitress: Compliments of the gentlemen sitting by the bar.

Carrie: You always get the best compliments.

Eileen: Well, I've heard of guys like that. I mean, look at him, the way he dresses, and the way he looks in the mirror like he admires himself. Without saying a word, I can already predict he does this all the time and he's a playboy.

Carrie: Really? But he seems nice.

Eileen: Don't be fooled by the wine and his innocent looks.

Carrie: I guess you're right. But without the wine, how else would he be able to meet us?

Eileen: I always follow my intuition to find a man. And this time my intuition tells me to stay away from that cheapskate.

Carrie: Really, your intuition tells you he's cheap?

Eileen: Well, sort of. You see this wine is the cheapest one on the menu. If he really wanted to pick us up, he should at least pick something a little pricier.

Carrie: Eileen, you are hopeless.

譯 對話譯點通

(Carrie和她女性的朋友Eileen，在餐廳用午餐，這時，有位女侍者送來紅酒。)

Eileen:	我們沒點紅酒啊！
Waitress:	這是坐在那兒的那位男士，對你的一點心意。
Carrie:	你總是得到最棒的恭維啊！
Eileen:	嗯，我知道那種人，我的意思是，你看看他，他穿的服裝，他照鏡子那種自戀的樣子。不用說，我已經猜到，他常常幹這種事，是個花花公子。
Carrie:	真的嗎？但是他看起來不錯ㄟ！
Eileen:	不要被他送來的酒，還有那付純真的樣子給騙了。
Carrie:	我想你說的對。但是如果沒有酒，他哪來機會跟我們照面？
Eileen:	我總是相信我的直覺去獵男，這次的直覺告訴我，遠離這個小氣鬼。
Carrie:	真的嗎，你的直覺告訴你他很小氣嗎？
Eileen:	嗯，不完全是。你看，這瓶酒是菜單上最便宜的酒，假如他真的想把我們，他至少該選貴一點的酒。
Carrie:	Eileen，你真是無藥可救了。

字 單字及片語

pick up	把上、釣（馬子／凱子）
In the meantime	同時間
order	v.點餐
compliment	n.恭維
playboy	n.花花公子
intuition	n.直覺
	同義字還有：
	instinct
	the sixth sense
	hunch
cheapskate	n.小氣鬼
You are hopeless.	你無藥可救了

> **Compliment of somebody**
> 指某人的致意

> 你還可以這樣說：dandy、ladykiller、womanizer。
> 美男子怎麼說呢？
> Casanova（Casanova是義大利人，據說是頂尖美男子，全名是：Casanova de seingalt Giocomo。）

愛情實戰
enjoy
享受

 CD 20

> **Dennis 小提醒：**
> 約會時，有人喜歡go Dutch（各付各的），有人喜歡treat（請客）。Go Dutch有暗諷荷蘭人非常吝嗇之嫌，為了不想讓荷蘭人太傷心，現在多用share代替go Dutch這個帶有偏見的英文了。

Dennis: Are you free Saturday evening?

Kelly: Well that depends on what you have in mind?

Dennis: How about a dinner, a movie, and maybe a bottle of red wine at my place afterwards?

Kelly: (smile) Dinner sounds great, I might go for the movie, too. But the red wine part seems a bit too fast for the first date.

Dennis: No problem, I'll pick you up at 6:00pm for dinner. How about Japanese?

Kelly: Great!

Dennis: For the movie, I'm thinking of the new Tom Cruise blockbuster.

Kelly: Excellent pick.

Dennis: And if you have a problem with the red wine, No problem, we'll have white.

Kelly: Ah...I think you missed my point!

譯 對話譯點通

Dennis: 妳星期六晚上有空嗎？

Kelly: 嗯，那得看你有啥計畫？

Dennis: 一起晚餐、看電影、也許之後到我家來杯紅酒，如何？

Kelly: （微笑）一起晚餐聽起來不錯，我也想看電影，但是紅酒部份，就第一次約會來說，好像太快了一點。

Dennis: 沒問題，那我六點來接你一起晚餐，日本料理好嗎？

Kelly: 很讚啊！

Dennis: 電影的話，我想到湯姆克魯斯最新的賣座片。

Kelly: 選的好！

Dennis: 那如果你對紅酒有意見，沒關係，我們可以選白酒！

Kelly: 嗯，我想你搞錯我的意思！

字 單字及片語

Are you free? =Are you available?	你有空嗎？
depend on	v.視…而定
pick up	v.接
	表示以交通工具接某人
blockbuster	n.賣座片
point	n.重點

還可以這樣說：

Are you busy on the 15th？
你十五號有空嗎？
What are you up to this weekend？
你週末要幹嘛？
What are you doing next weekend？
你下週有空嗎？
Would you like to go out to dinner？
你想不想吃晚餐？
Would you like to......
很客氣的說法，能給人好印象。

享受番外篇
Dennis**心法傳授**
營造浪漫約會

我和**Judy**的公路旅遊，其實就是要營造浪漫約會。怎麼營造呢？首先，要選美景。

我和**Judy**的浪漫之旅，來到美國加州最美的海岸 Monterey Bay，這裡同時是我的家鄉，閃閃發光的海面，聚集了成群的沙丁魚，岸邊有海獅（sea lion），天邊有海鷗（sea gull）、漁人碼頭上有鵜鶘（pelican），鵜鶘是 Monterey Bay 常見的一種海鳥。

因為景色太美，光是坐在那裡看漁人抓沙丁魚，時間就過兩個小時。我們就在那裡凝視，在別人眼中，一定呈現一種痴呆的傻樣。（哈）

除了漁人碼頭，我們還走進了全世上最大的水族館，發亮的水母、成群各式各樣的海洋生物…兩人玩得不亦樂乎。

離開「Monterey Bay」，我們來到旅程的終點：「Santa Cruz」，這裡有伴隨我成長的海灘。剛剛提過約會要先有美景，之後，要把戰線拉到自己擅長的領域。所以大家知道了，這片沙灘就是我的地盤，我當然不會輕易放棄任何展現的機會。

於是，一個體格良好、擁有著結實六塊肌的年輕男子（就是我）冒著零度左右的水溫（雖然天氣很好，但是海洋流域的溫度還是很低），順著線條極佳的海浪，我充分展現了衝浪的本領！這一切的表現，只為一搏佳人一笑。（她的確笑了，而且大笑，因為上來後我抖得要死，嘴唇發紫。）

愛情實戰
living together
同居

 CD 21

> **Dennis 小提醒：**
> 熱戀後想當然爾會想同居，其實熱戀有很多不同的層次：**They have been in love with each other for years.** 指兩人相戀多年。熱戀時形影不離：**They are two peas in a pod.**（他們像豆莢裡的兩粒豆子），熱戀時目中無人：**They only have eyes for each other.**（世上似乎只有他們兩人）。

Yvette: Have you heard that Emily moved into Tom's house last week?

Dennis: Well it's about time.

Yvette: They've been together forever. I think it's great that they are taking this relationship to the next level.

Dennis: I agree, I think it's about time they saved some rent.

Yvette: What do you mean?

Dennis: Well even though they weren't living together, but they were always staying over at each other's apartments. Why pay the extra rent?

Yvette: You've got a point there, but I think moving their relationship to the next level sounds so much better.

對話譯點通

Yvette: 你聽說Emily上週搬進Tom的住處了嗎？

Dennis: 嗯，終於。

Yvette: 他們在一起很久囉，他們決定要讓彼此的關係進入下一個階段，我覺得很好啊。

Dennis: 我同意，我想也是節省租金的時候了。

Yvette: 你說什麼？

Dennis: 對啊，即使他們沒有住在一起，他們總是留在對方的住處過夜，幹嘛要付額外的租金？

Yvette: 你說對了，但我還是覺得，把它想成要讓關係更進一步，聽起來會好很多。

 單字及片語

move into	搬進
It's about time.	時間上來說，也差不多了。在對話中表示「終於」的意思。
level	n.階段
stay over	v.過夜
even though	即使…
each other's	adj.彼此的
extra	adj.多餘的
rent	n.租金
It sounds so much better.	聽起來好多了

愛情實戰

on the bed
床上

Dennis 情色小提醒：
「你們上床了嗎？」問法有很多：Did you do it？
Did you sleep together？Did you make it？
Did you go all the way？Did you score？另外
還有，「Did you get any action？」action＝
sex，這裡指的是性愛喲。

Dennis: Was it good for you as it was for me?

Mary: It was great!

Dennis: I don't think I deserve all the credit. I thought you were great, too.

Mary: I think we make a good team. I mean when you were pushing and I was pulling, I just thought that was perfect.

Dennis: Well, I personally loved that part when you were in front and I was behind you, it was almost like we were acting as one.

Mary: you were great.

Dennis: No, you were great, too.

Mary: I would never want to move my mattress with any other friend but you.

Dennis: I now officially announce that Mary is my mattress moving partner for life.

Mary: With all that moving the mattress around, want to get on the mattress and do some more moving?

Dennis: I thought you'd never ask. Now just want to make sure, did you like me pushing or pulling, or in front, or behind, or is it......

Mary: Just shut up and get your butt in bed now.

譯 對話譯點通

Dennis: 你跟我感覺一樣棒嗎？

Mary: 很棒啊！

Dennis: 我不認為全是我的功勞，我想你也很棒。

Mary: 我想我們默契絕佳，我的意思是，你一推我一拉，感覺很完美。

Dennis: 嗯，我個人偏愛，你前面我後面，好像我們已合而為一。

Mary: 你剛剛真的很棒。

Dennis: 沒有啦，你才棒。

Mary: 除了你之外，我不會跟別人一起搬床墊。

Dennis: 我現在正式宣佈，Mary是我生命當中搬床墊的最伙伴。

Mary: 我們床墊搬來搬去，要不要真的到床墊上動一動？

Dennis: 我以為你不會開口哩，現在只要告訴我，你要進出，還是前面或是後面，還是…

Mary: 閉嘴，滾上床來。

 單字及片語

deserve	v.值得
credit	n.榮耀
personally	adv.個人地
mattress	n.床墊
officially	adv.官方地、正式地
announce	v.宣布、發布
shut up	v.閉嘴
butt	n.屁股，bottom的口語化說法

愛情實戰
sweet words
甜言蜜語

CD 23

Dennis: I love you.

Mary: I love you, too.

Dennis: I love you with all my heart.

Mary: I've loved you with every cell in my body.

Dennis: I can't live without you. You make me feel so special.

Mary: If I have to live without you, I think someone should call an ambulance and bring plenty of oxygen tanks.

Dennis: I'm not sure I follow.

Mary: Well, without you I would go to Tibet and become a monk. But I heard you should bring plenty of oxygen due to the high altitude.

Dennis: I think we've blown this way out of proportion. Let's just start from scratch, I love you.

Mary: I love you, too. And...

Dennis: Stop right there, just a simple I love you will do just fine. Remember, more is not always more, but less is always more.

對話譯點通

Dennis: 我愛妳。
Mary: 我也愛你。
Dennis: 我全心全意的愛妳。
Mary: 我身上每個毛細孔都愛你。
Dennis: 沒有妳我活不下去，妳讓我覺得自己如此特別。
Mary: 假如生活中沒有了你，我想應該有人叫救護車，給我很多的氧氣筒。
Dennis: 我好像不知道你在說什麼。
Mary: 真的，沒有了你，我可能會去西藏當僧侶。但是那裡海拔這樣高，我覺得你應該帶氧氣筒給我。
Dennis: 我覺得現在的狀況太誇張了而且想太多了，讓我們重頭來，我愛你。
Mary: 我也愛你，還有…
Dennis: 停，可以打住了，只要說簡單的「我愛你」三個字就夠了。記住，多未必是多，少總是多。

 單字及片語

ambulance	n.救護車
plenty of +複數N	很多，後面加複數名詞
oxygen	n.氧氣
tank	n.貯存氧氣的筒罐
follow	v.追隨
Tibet	n.西藏
monk	n.僧侶
blow	v.吹牛、自誇，過去分詞blown
out of proportion	破了比例，表示已經夠了
scratch	v.挖、扒　n.起跑線
start from scratch	重頭來

愛情實戰

giving presents
送禮

CD 24

Dennis: Hello?

Jessie: Guess what I have behind my back. Tada!

Dennis: You got me a present! How nice and may I ask what this is for?

Jessie: It's our fourth year anniversary, don't tell me you forgot!

Dennis: I I I I I I I ....I didn't, How could you possible accuse me of forgetting our anniversary?

Jessie: Well if you didn't forget, where is my present?

Dennis: You see, my present doesn't fit behind my back or in my pocket. I got you something bigger.

Jessie: Something bigger? I can't wait. Where is it? oh it's in the garage!

Dennis: Tada!! A set of golf clubs.

Jessie: I don't know how to play golf.

Dennis: What a great time to learn.

Jessie: But it's got your initials on it.

Dennis: Well, that's because the next time we play golf, I will carry the bag for you so the caddies need to know my name. Just to make sure, I have taken your clubs and played a few games already, to be certain that everything works properly.

Jessie: So it's used, too? Dennis, that is the worst lie I have ever heard of. You will get into your car and drive to the Tiffany's shop and pick something you think I will like. If you're not back in an hour or you picked something I don't like, I will personally go back to that store with your credit card and buy myself a real present. I suggest you fix this situation when you have this chance, because if I go back with your credit card, I have a feeling that we may see tears in your eyes tonight.

譯 對話譯點通

Dennis: 哈囉！

Jessie: 猜猜看我後面有什麼？噹噹！

Dennis: 你給我的禮物。真好，我可以問為何送我禮物嗎？

Jessie: 我們結婚四週年紀念，不要告訴我你忘了喔。

Dennis: 我我我我…我沒忘啊，你怎麼會指控我忘記結婚紀念日呢？

Jessie: 好啊，如果你沒忘記，那我的禮物在哪裡？

Dennis: 妳看，我準備的禮物藏不了我的身後也放不進我的口袋，就表示，我準備了大大的禮物要送給妳。

Jessie: 大大的禮物？我等不及了。在哪裡？喔，一定在車庫。

Dennis: 噹噹，一組高爾夫球桿。

Jessie: 我不會打高爾夫球啊。

Dennis: 正好可以學哩。

Jessie: 上面有你的名字哩！

Dennis: 嗯，因為下次我們打高爾夫球，我幫你拿球桿，所以桿弟需要知道我的名字，為了確定沒有什麼問題，我已經先拿妳的球桿打了幾場，只是為了確定一切都沒問題。

Jessie: 所以，這是用過的囉？ Dennis，這是我聽過最扯的謊言，你現在立刻上車，把車開到Tiffany珠寶店，選幾款你覺得我會喜歡的禮物。假如你一小時沒回來或是你選到了我不喜歡的東西，我就要拿你的信用卡，自己到那家店犒賞我自己個好禮物。我建議你好好把握機會收拾殘局，因為如果我帶著你的信用卡去的話，我覺得你晚上會哭出來。

字 單字及片語

tada	n.噹噹，擬聲辭
what...for	做什麼用
accuse	v.控訴
golf club	n.高爾夫球桿
initial	adj.最初的　n.起首，最初，這裡表示姓名的首字母
caddie	n.高爾夫球球僮
fix this situation	收拾殘局

愛情實戰

long distance relationship
遠距戀情

 CD 25

Dennis: I can't believe you let your boyfriend study abroad. Isn't it very hard to maintain a long distance relationship?

Amy: I just don't have the heart to stop him from pursuing his dream.

Dennis: In a long distance relationship, you don't know where he's at all time, who he's out with , or what they are talking about.

Amy: It's ok. I have you to take care of me when he's not around.

Dennis: That brings me to my next point. Since your boyfriend is not around, I will be honest with you. I have had feelings for you since the first day we met. But your boyfriend has always been in the equation. Now that he's gone, you think you can take a closer look at me and maybe give me a shot?

Amy: My boyfriend just left 2 days ago!

Dennis: Well if the feeling is mutual, why wait?

Amy: I'm going to need some time to think this through.

Dennis: Great, I'll pick you up at 7:00pm and we'll think things through over dinner.

Amy: Eric, you're the best friend anyone could ever have.

Dennis: Besides your overseas boyfriend, I can be your best friend in the world.

Dennis (thinking to himself): And I just got a first date with Amy......I'm good!

譯 對話譯點通

Dennis: 我不知道為什麼妳讓男友出國留學，要維繫遠距離戀情可不容易呢？

Amy: 我只是不想阻止他去追尋自己的夢想。

Dennis: 談遠距戀愛，妳不知道他大部分時間在哪裡？他跟誰出去？他們談了什麼？

Amy: 沒關係啊，當他不在身邊，我還有你照顧我。

Dennis: 這就說到我下一個重點了。因為你男朋友不在，我要誠實的告訴你，自從我們第一天見面，我就對你有感覺，但一直礙於你有男朋友的狀況。現在他不在了，妳可以再多看看我，給我機會嗎？

Amy: 我男友才離開兩天耶。

Dennis: 嗯，假如這感覺雙方都有，為何要等呢？

Amy: 我會花一些時間去想想。

Dennis: 好啊，我七點來接你，我們晚餐時間都可以想。

Amy: Eric，你真是我最好的朋友了。

Dennis: 除了你那留學海外的男友之外，我是你這世界上最好的朋友。

Dennis(心裡偷偷想): 我剛搞定我跟Amy的第一次約會，我真厲害！

字 單字及片語

pursue	v.追求
at all time	一直，始終
equation	n.方程式
Your boyfriend has always been in the equation.	equation，方程式。
mutual	adj.互相的
overseas	adj.海外的

> 方程式指的是一個狀況，當用equation來形容人事物的時候，指的就是：是否在狀況內。

愛情實戰

parking
車震，停車

 CD 26

Cindy: Hey, I saw a movie called "A rebel without a cause" over the weekend and I loved it.

Dennis: Wow, I haven't heard that name in a long time. That has got to be one of Hollywood's best classics. And James Dean, I think he's an icon who everymen wants to be and everywoman wants to be with, type of movie star.

Cindy: I noticed an interesting term in there where all the students wanted to go park by the lake.

Dennis: That term was probably made popular in the 50's or 60's but it seems like it's making a comeback recently.

Cindy: What do you mean "making a comeback"? People have always been parking their cars.

Dennis: Well, you see the term used in the movie "go parking with someone" means finding a place romantic, park your car there.......

Cindy: And?

Dennis: And you do the wild thing in the car.

Cindy: What? But it's so tiny, cluttered, and the chair, the gear shift... What if someone sees you?

Dennis: Well I guess that's part of the fun. When you are in love with someone anywhere can be romantic. And besides for a teenager, that car may be the most comfortable place they've got.

Cindy: I guess when you are young, crazy and wild are a part of the package.

Dennis: So Cindy, want to go parking with me up on the mountain?

Cindy: Give it a rest, old man.

對話譯點通

Cindy: 嘿，我週末看了部電影，叫做「養子不教誰之過」，我愛死了。

Dennis: 哇，好久沒聽到這部電影了，這是好萊塢經典名片之一。男主角詹姆斯狄恩（James Dean），是那種每個男人都想成為他，每個女人都想擁有他的電影明星。

Cindy: 我注意到一個有趣的説法：學生都要去湖邊停車？

Dennis: 那個詞在50或60年代很流行，但是最近似乎又流行回來了。

Cindy: 你説流行回來是什麼意思啊，停車是一直都有的事啊。

Dennis: 嗯，妳看喔，這字在電影中的意思是：和某人去停車，意思是找個羅曼蒂克的地方，把車停在那裡···

Cindy: 然後？

Dennis: 然後在車上作瘋狂的事。

Cindy: 什麼？但是車上那麼擁擠、雜亂、有椅子、有排擋器…假如有人看到怎麼辦？

Dennis: 嗯，我想這是樂趣的一部分。　當你和某人戀愛，任何地方都很羅曼蒂克。而且，對青少年來説，車子是他們最舒適的地方了。

Cindy: 我想，年輕時，瘋狂和狂野總是分不開。

Dennis: 所以，Cindy，要跟我去山上停車嗎？

Cindy: 休想，你這老頭。

 單字及片語

in a long time	好久了
classics	n.經典
make a comeback	重整其鼓，意指流行回來
tiny	adj.微小的
cluttered	adj.亂七八糟的
gear shift	n.排擋器
go parking with someone	車震，與某人在車上發生性關係
teenager	n.青少年
a part of the package	整組之一，分不開
give it a rest	得了吧，別想了，休想的意思

愛情實戰
poetic
詩意的

Lyrics... Your song
It's a little bit funny
This feeling inside
It's not one of those you can easily hide
I know it's not much but it's the best I can do
My gift is my song and this one's for you
You can tell everybody this is your song
It may be quite simple but now that it's done
I hope you don't mind I hope you don't mind
that I put down in words
How wonderful life is while you're in the world

Dennis: Poetry and love seems to always fit together so perfectly.

Sofia: I can't agree with you more.

Dennis: You know I'm sort of a love poet myself.

Sofia: Really? I didn't know you had it in you.

Dennis: "Roses are red and violets are blue. You're the hottest chick ever, and I wanna be with you." I was thinking of sending it into some publisher because I've got many more. Do you want to hear them?

Sofia: Dennis, I don't know how to tell you this but keep the day job.

對話譯點通

歌詞（你的歌）

這有點好笑

這種感覺在心中

這不是一個容易隱藏的感覺

我知道這不多但這是我能盡力去做的

我的禮物是要送你我的歌

妳可以告訴大家這是屬於你的歌

也許有點簡短但是已經完成了

我希望你別介意我寫的詞

你的存在讓世界真美好

Dennis: 詩和愛似乎總是如此完美的組合在一起。

Sofia: 我很贊同你的說法。

Dennis: 你知道我自己也是個愛情詩人。

Sofia: 真的嗎？我不知道你有這方面的天分。

Dennis: 「玫瑰是紅色，紫羅蘭是藍色；你是最辣的女孩，我想
永遠跟你在一起。」，我老想把這寄給出版商，我的創
作源源不絕，還有很多耶，你想聽嗎？

Sofia: Dennis，我不知道怎麼跟你說，但是先別把你的工作辭掉。

 單字及片語

the best I can do	盡全力做到最好
put down	v.寫下
poetry	n.詩歌
chick	小雞，這裡指的是女孩。
publisher	n.出版者
I've got many more.	我有很多，指作品很多，創意源源不絕。
keep the day job	字面上的意思是：先別把工作辭掉，暗指別轉行。

愛情實戰

lovers pledges
海誓山盟

 CD 28

Grace: I went to a friend's wedding over the weekend and it was the most beautiful wedding I have ever attended.

Dennis: Really? I never thought of you as the marrying type.

Grace: Are you kidding? I can't wait for that Mr. Right to show up in my life and the perfect wedding that I've always dreamed of..... Can you do me a favor?

Dennis: What?

Grace: Can you say the wedding vows to me?

Dennis: Are you serious?

Grace: Oh please...I just want to feel that moment. Come on, be a friend.

Dennis: I will love you for better or for worse, happiness or sadness, for rich or poor, through health or sickness till death do us part.

Grace: Wow, those are the magic words.

Dennis: I think you desperately need of a man.

Grace: I am.

Dennis: I'm available!

Grace: Not that desperate.

譯 對話譯點通

Grace: 我週末去參加一個朋友的婚禮，那是我所參加過的婚禮中最漂亮的一場婚禮了。

Dennis: 真的？我沒想過你是會結婚那一型的。

Grace: 你開玩笑吧，我等不及哪個對的男人出現在我的生命中，而且我總是夢想有一場完美的婚禮…你可以幫我個忙嗎？

Dennis: 什麼忙？

Grace: 你可以對我說婚姻誓言嗎？

Dennis: 你是認真的嗎？

Grace: 真的啦！請說…我想感覺那一刻，快點，是朋友的話。

Dennis: 我愛你，不管好或壞，快樂或悲傷，富貴或貧窮，健康或病苦，直到死亡將我們拆散。

Grace: 哇，真是神奇的語言。

Dennis: 我想妳迫切的需要一個男人。

Grace: 我是啊！

Dennis: 我有空。

Grace: 我還沒那樣迫切。

字 單字及片語

attend	v.參加
marrying type	結婚那一型
show up	v.出現
do me a favor	幫我個忙
Are you serious?	你是認真的嗎？也可以簡單說seriously？
vow	n.誓言　v.發誓
till death do us part	直至死亡把我們分開
desperately	adv.迫切地，形容詞desperate，迫切的。
available	adj.可用的、有空的

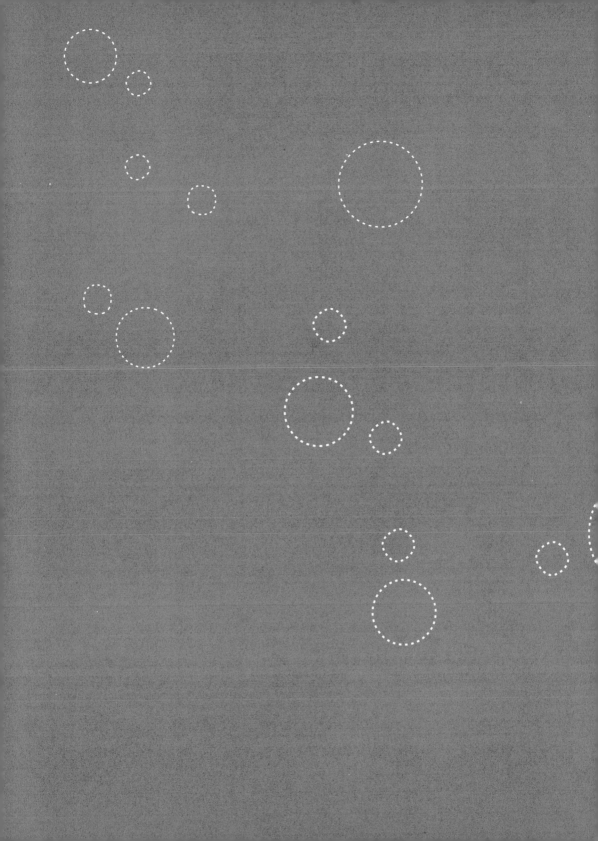

我談的那場戀愛 . . .

　　18歲的時候，我認識了一位讓我至今難忘的女孩，她的名字叫Emily。怎麼說「難忘」呢？我和她，有過最甜蜜，卻也最充滿負荷的一段愛情。

　　我記得認識她是在一次party，當時陌生與熟悉的朋友聚在一起，大家杯光交錯。酒意方酣時，我帶著一點微醺的醉意，遇見了Emily。她向我走來，臉上掛著迷人的笑容，稱不上是大美女，但已經算是我們這群狐朋狗友，公認最具魅力的女孩了！那時宴會接近尾聲，心機重的我卡了一個好位子，成為護送她回家的第一人選。回家的路上，我極盡所能展現自己的幽默（還有博學！），她回報以欣羨，略帶仰慕的眼光，我暗爽在心頭：強敵環伺的追求者中，我已略佔上風。

　　我還記得當天晚上，我送她到家後，第二天為了確認她家的正確位置，還特地再開車去一次，為往後的「接送」與「不期而遇」做好準備。上天眷顧有心人，極其順利的，我們很快成了一對戀人，也同時開展日後最難忘的時光。

　　老實說，Emily是體貼入微的好情人，她無微不至的細心照顧，讓我像備受寵愛的孩子，甚至有點受寵若驚。每天早上起床，她會費心準備早餐溫暖地向我說早安，下課鐘響，她溫柔地等在我的教室旁。不僅為我準備生日禮物，還為我的朋友準備昂貴精緻的贈禮，她的細心讓我五體投地。

　　好吧！我承認，最初看見她這一切愛的表示，我真的非常感動。但是久了，感受到一種隱形的壓力。每回學期末，她會拿出下學期的課表要我照表抄課（意思是選同樣的課），我們便能形影不離。漸漸，我身邊的空氣開始變得稀薄，開始失去獨處的時間和空間，甚至，連上個廁所，都有她在門外等候！同時，朋友的聚會開始變成請求，每當我想和朋友哈拉打屁，Emily都能以完美的修辭一一駁回，由於她高超的說服技巧、俐落的分析能力，她總讓我相信：她的安排是最棒的！

天生反骨的我，漸漸受不住這樣的高壓控管，就算以愛為名，還是會有想逃脫的念頭。當抗拒開始出現，我才驚覺，昔日的天使已成魔鬼。接下來：衝突、爭吵不斷，如漫天落下的冰雹，讓我至今心有餘悸。

其實情人間的爭吵應該是家常便飯，有時候來個 Kiss and make up.（親一下，和好吧！）事情就可以解決了。但是集天使與魔鬼一身的Emily，用的是令人難以招架的軟硬兼施。為了達到她的目的，她能充滿毅力拉長戰線，從教室到家裡，從客廳到廚房，最兇狠一次，是她以肉身擋住我欲離開的車身，雙眼炯炯，好像要跟我決鬥，我的所有道歉，在她的氣頭上，都化為烏有。

經過與Emily交手後，我逐漸有了覺悟。基本上我以為，男人根本不該和女人吵架，不吵架不是因為沒有爭端或歧見，而是：「根本吵不贏！」多數的男人，像個粗心的大孩子，當我們還傻傻的停在今天的事件，女人已經在腦海統計過去的爭吵和分析未來的局面，一旦細數好了如散彈掃射過來，舊愁加新怨，事情的焦點就混淆了。

儘管不捨，這段感情終究隨著一次又一次的爭吵慢慢消失，這場戀情前後持續了兩年，我和Emily的愛情，最終在分分合合的爭吵中劃下句點。

♥ 浪漫小語

Kiss and make up!（親一下，和好吧！）

這是常發生在情人爭吵之後的調皮用法，「我們不要吵架了，來親一個！」可能帶點哄的味道，但多半女孩都吃這套。不過我的建議是，誤會還是需要解釋清楚，多一點包容與體貼，再來句「Kiss and make up」，就能緩解紛爭，繼續徜徉在甜蜜的情海裡。

愛情實戰
flirt
調情

Carol: I can't stand people who flirt. I think it shows that they mess around and they don't take anything seriously.

Dennis: Do you think I flirt?

Carol: Come on, you are the biggest flirt I know. Not only do you flirt with the girls that are after you, but you even flirt with girls at the fast food counter.

Dennis: But she was so cute!

Carol: All I'm trying to say is that if you really like someone then like them. If you don't like them, don't flirt and lead them on.

Dennis: I guess I'm the type of person that would not jump into a pool without knowing the water conditions.

Carol: I'm not sure I follow.

Dennis: What I'm saying is that by flirting, I'm testing out the water temperature. If it doesn't feel right, I won't stick my neck out there.

Carol: Love is something special, when you find the right person you should be bold, be brave, be daring and don't show your affection so lightly.

Dennis: I take love very seriously, that's why I flirt with people and in the process I try to find the right one. And in the process, I'm having a blast.

對話譯點通

Carol:	我不能忍受別人調情，我覺得這樣好像亂來，而且不當一回事。
Dennis:	你覺得我有跟人家調情嗎？
Carol:	拜託，你是我所認識的人當中最會調情的，在速食店，你不但跟後面的人調情，甚至還跟櫃檯前的人調情。
Dennis:	但是她真的很可愛。
Carol:	我只是想說，如果你真的喜歡某個人，那去喜歡吧，如果你不喜歡，那請不要調情、惹人家。
Dennis:	我覺得我好像是那種，不知道泳池狀況不跳進去的那種人。
Carol:	我不知道你在說什麼。
Dennis:	我要說的是，藉著調情，我測試水的溫度，如果感覺苗頭不對，我不會跳進去。
Carol:	愛是很珍貴的，當你發現某個對的人，你應該鼓起勇氣、大膽，勇於實踐，不要怯於表達情感。
Dennis:	我很認真去看待愛這件事啊，所以我才會跟別人調情，從調情的過程中，我試著去發現對的人，而且在這個過程中，我玩得很盡興呢！

 單字及片語

can't stand	不能忍受
mess around	亂來、亂搞
take....seriously	對...認真
not only....but (also可省略)...	不僅...而且...，not only放在前面，後面動詞需要倒裝
flirt with+人	和某人調情
lead on	v.帶領，在對話中表示去招惹的意思。
I'm not sure I follow.	我不知道你在說什麼。
temperature	n.溫度
stick	v. 貼
bold	adj. 大膽的 (bold，brave，daring這裡都是形容詞，勇敢的意思。)
affection	n.情感
lightly	輕微的、少量的
in the process	過程中
I'm having a blast.	我玩得很盡興，blast是爆炸、狂歡的意思

愛情實戰
fight
爭吵

CD 30

(Sofia is having a huge fight with her boyfriend, Dennis.)

Sofia: I hate fighting because it hurts a relationship, it makes your blood pressure go up and I simply think I look prettier when I'm not angry.

Dennis: You're right, I hate arguing, too. In fact I hate it more than you do because it makes a person say awful things that you can't take back and it really brings out the worst in you.

Sofia: I can't agree with you more, but I really doubt you can hate fighting more than I, cause I'm just the most peaceful person in the world.

Dennis: No No No, I think you are on the right track except for one little detail, that I'm the most peaceful person there is.

Sofia: Whatever, I dislike fighting way more than you and there is nothing you can say that will change that fact.

Dennis: Sure, Sofia ...I don't want to fight with you. Whatever you say, I just want to get one point across, I'm more easy going.

Sofia: No, I am.

Dennis: No, I am.

Sofia: I am ....

譯 對話譯點通

（ Sofia 和他的男友 Dennis 起了爭執 ）

Sofia: 我討厭吵架，因為這會破壞兩人的關係。吵架會使你血壓升高，而我只要不生氣，就會覺得自己漂亮許多。

Dennis: 你說的對，我也很討厭吵架。事實上，我比你更討厭吵架，因為吵架會讓人說惡毒的話，而那些話收不回來，而且對你帶來傷害。

Sofia: 我很同意你。但是我真懷疑你比我更厭惡吵架，因為我是這世界上最愛好和平的人了。

Dennis: 不不不，我覺得你是對的，除了有個小地方：我才是這世界上最愛好和平的人了。

Sofia: 不管怎樣，我比你更不喜歡吵架，而且這是不可改變的事實。

Dennis: 當然，Sofia....我不想跟你吵架。不管你說啥，我只有一個重點，我的個性比較隨和。

Sofia: 不，我才是。

Dennis: 不，我才是。

Sofia: 我才是....

 字 單字及片語

fight	v.爭吵
huge	adj.巨大的
blood pressure	n.血壓
argue	v.爭吵
take back	v.收回
brings out the worst in you	對你帶來傷害
I can't agree with you more.	我非常贊成你
on the right track	走在對的路上
easy going	表示個性隨和

爭吵番外篇

聶雲心法傳授

怎樣分手？

　　面對一個擁有多年感情的戀人，要將分手說出口，不是件容易的事。於是，熟悉的爭吵如同迴圈，分分合合，譜成了最終離別的前奏曲。耐人尋味的是，「make up sex」竟也成了每回衝突的高潮點，爭吵、口角，好像都是為了後面的激情作準備，聽起來既煽情又曖昧！

　　「The best part about breaking up is making up afterwards.」（分手後最棒的是接下來的激情）這是國外朋友耳熟能詳的一句話。外國人的性觀念比較開放，對身體的交互運動與感應，比較無所避諱，那怕是爭吵的面紅耳赤，或許在下一秒，一場蓄勢待發的激情即將上演！但是我勸大家少用為妙，重口味的方式雖然刺激，但很容易不再有效。

　　分手時，地點的選擇很重要。首先，請避免浪漫的地方，比如：過去兩人經常一起去的地方，那太容易觸景生情了。再來，不要選擇太偏僻的場所，幽密場所像私會。簡單的說，公眾或人群聚集的場所，是分手最好的

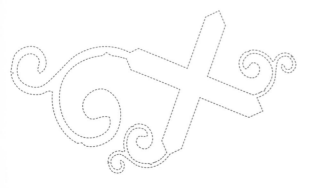

點，比如：擾攘的街頭啦、**coffee shop** 啦、速食餐廳啦，愈是不隱密的地方，愈是安全。

　　分手的過程，最好是和諧而充滿溫暖的。畢竟相識一場，或許多年以後，偶然在街頭相遇，約著去輕啜一杯咖啡，回憶一些舊事，都能讓所有甜蜜的過往定格在最美的瞬間！

愛情實戰
have an affair
劈腿

Christine: I slept with my ex-boyfriend last night.

Dennis: Are you having an affair?

Christine: No, it was just one of those heat of the moment things, you know, booty call.

Dennis: Ok, just that once right? Although it's not right, everyone makes mistakes. Don't be so hard on yourself.

Christine: Yes, just that once in his house ... And the other time in his office.

Dennis: That's twice, you are having an affair!

Christine: And the time he came over to my apartment, and when I drove him home in my car, and, oh my God you're right I am having an affair. What am I going to do?

Dennis: Well you better figure something out, cause you know what they say, three is always a crowd.

Christine: You're right. I am in so much trouble.

Dennis: Yes, you are. So tell me was it worth it?

Christine: You know what, it was great... Ha Ha Ha

Dennis: You're such a bad girl.

譯 對話譯點通

Christine:	昨晚我和我前男友上床了！
Dennis:	妳在搞劈腿嗎？
Christine:	沒有！不過就是那天雷勾動地火的一剎那罷了，人的本能嘛！
Dennis:	好吧！只有那一次嗎？雖然這樣很不應該，但是每個人都會犯錯，你也不要太自責。
Christine:	是的，就那一次，在他家……另一次在他辦公室。
Dennis:	那是兩次了，你已經劈腿了！
Christine:	還有那次，他到我住的地方，還有一次我載他回家，在我車上……還有，啊！我的天，你說對了，我已經劈腿了。我該怎麼辦？
Dennis:	好吧，你最好趕快想個辦法，因為你知道別人總是說，三人行是太擁擠了些。
Christine:	你說的對，我真是有大麻煩了。
Dennis:	是啊，告訴我，你覺得這樣做值得嗎？
Christine:	你知道嗎，那真的好棒…哈哈哈。
Dennis:	你真是個壞女孩。

字 單字及片語

have an affair	指劈腿或外遇
one of +複數N	其中之一，後面一定要用複數名詞。
booty call	booty call是俚語，意思是，某人想跟你嘿咻的一通電話或訊息，這裡指的是「人的本能反應」的意思。
once	a.一次、一回，也可作為「一旦、曾經」的用法。
You (had) better...	你最好... 縮寫you'd better。口語化會直接講You better...
figure out	v.理解、想出
in trouble	有麻煩

> 例如：It is said that he was once a thief. 聽說他曾做過小偷。

愛情實戰
cheating
偷腥

 CD 32

Dennis: I think cheating is an art.

Jasmine: I'm sorry, I am not sure I understand you.

Dennis: Well, cheating won't exist unless one is caught.

Jasmine: You say that because you cheat.

Dennis: No, I am serious. Cheating is like Hide and Seek; one couldn't exist without the other.

Jasmine: What is this, the theory of moral relativity.

Dennis: Maybe it is!

對話譯點通

Dennis:	我認為偷腥是個藝術。
Jasmine:	我很抱歉，我不確定我了解你的意思！
Dennis:	嗯，偷腥這件事是直到被逮到了才算存在的。
Jasmine:	你這樣說是因為你自己就在偷腥！
Dennis:	不，我說真的。偷腥就像「抓迷藏」，一個巴掌拍不響的。
Jasmine:	這根本就是道德相對論！
Dennis:	或許就是吧！

 單字及片語

cheat	v.作弊、偷腥
exist	v.存在
I am serious.	我是認真的（用來強調自己嚴肅的態度）
Hidden and Seek	n.躲迷藏，一種遊戲。
moral	adj.道德的
relativity	n.相對論
until	直到
is caught	被發現，英語的被動式，動詞原型要改為過去分詞喔！ catch的分詞:caught
maybe	adv.大概、或許

愛情實戰
one-night stand
一夜情

Lydia: Hey, Dennis, Have you had a one-night stand before?

Dennis: Well, that's a secret.

Lydia: Well, I had an one last night and it was awful.

Dennis: How?

Lydia: Well, the night wasn't too bad, but in the morning...... the guy looked nothing like the person I met in the bar the night before and he had very bad breath.

Dennis: Fortunately, that was just one night. Look on the bright side, that's the beauty of a one-night stand, you don't ever have to see him again.

Lydia: Look at the facts, that's one night too many.

對話譯點通

Lydia: 嘿！Dennis，你有沒有過一夜情的經驗？

Dennis: 嗯！那是秘密！

Lydia: 好吧！我昨晚有一次相當糟的經驗！

Dennis: 怎麼説？

Lydia: 是啦！那晚還不賴！但是早上起來，那傢伙和我前晚在夜店碰到的簡直是不一樣的人，而且，他還有口臭。

Dennis: 幸好，那只是一晚！從好處想，那也是浪漫一夜情的好處，你從此不會再看到他了。

Lydia: 實際上，這表示連那一個晚上都是多餘的。

 單字及片語

one-night stand	n.一夜情
awful	adj.可怕的
the night before	前晚
bad breath	口臭
fortunately	adv.幸運地、好運地
look on the bright side	從好處想、從光明面看

愛情實戰
heart-broken
心碎

 CD 34

> **Dennis 小提醒:**
> heart-broken 指心被傷透了的狀態,用作名詞使用。
> 比方你可以說,**I had my heart-broken**。(我也曾
> 有傷心的往事)而 **break one's heart** 指(傷了誰的
> 心),**break** 用作動詞使用。

Dennis: How's it going? What's going on with that new guy you're seeing, David, right?

Judy: I don't know, he seems like a great person. But it's so hard for me to accept him.

Dennis: Why, what's wrong?

Judy: I just don't think I'm over my last relationship yet. My heart was broken and I don't want to get hurt again.

Dennis: I know it can be hard picking up the pieces of your broken heart, but you can't live in the past. This is a new relationship, you should know that it's always better to have loved wrong than to have never loved at all.

Judy: You're right. I'm going to give it a shot.

Dennis: That's the spirit.

譯 對話譯點通

Dennis: 最近如何？你和那個新交往的男生狀況如何？他叫David，是吧？

Judy: 我不知道，他似乎是個很棒的人，但我很難接受他。

Dennis: 為何？哪裡不對勁嗎？

Judy: 我只是覺得我的上一段感情好像還沒結束。我的心碎了，我不想再受到傷害。

Dennis: 我知道破碎的心要一片片補起來可能很困難，不過你不能一直活在過去。這是一段新感情，你應該了解，寧可愛錯，不要沒有愛過。

Judy: 你說的對，我要把過去拋在腦後。

Dennis: 這才對嘛！

字 單字及片語

How's it going?	最近如何？(還可以這樣說：What's up)
What's going on...	進行的怎樣？
it's so hard for me...	對我來說很困難
What's wrong?	哪裡有問題嗎？
get hurt again	再度受傷
pick up	拾起
live in the past	v.活在過去
not (never)...at all	一點也不，通常用於否定句
give it a shot	v.讓它消失、拋開
That's the spirit.	這才對！

例如：I don't like her at all.
(我一點也不喜歡她。)

愛情實戰
shackle
桎梏、枷鎖

CD 35

Dennis: Let's make up.

Jennifer: you mean let's forgive and forget?

Dennis: Yeah, you've got me. I was wrong and I made a mistake. Can we patch things up and be together again? I love you and I know you are the best thing that's ever happened to me.

Jennifer: You're right, you were wrong, and I am the best thing that's ever happened to you. But no, there is no way I am going to patch things up again.

Dennis: Calm down, will you?

Jennifer: No, you calm down. You had your chance and you were too stupid to see a good thing even if it smacked you in the face. I have had it with you and your shackles around my ankle. I am a free women, I feel great, and I am not about to make the same mistake twice.

Dennis: Can't we talk it over?

Jennifer: Out of my sight, you loser!

Dennis: So... is that a "No"?

譯 對話譯點通

Dennis: 我們和好吧！

Jennifer: 你的意思是說原諒和遺忘？

Dennis: 對，被你說中了。我錯了，我犯了錯誤，我們可以不要去計較，重修舊好嗎？我愛你，而且我知道，你是發生在我生命當中最美好的事。

Jennifer: 你說的對，你做錯了，我是你生命中最美好的事情。但是，很抱歉，我不可能再跟你重修舊好。

Dennis: 妳可不可以冷靜下來？

Jennifer: 不，你才需要冷靜。你有過機會，你笨到就算好東西丟在你臉上你都看不到，我受夠被你套牢了。我現在是一個自由的女人，這感覺很棒，我不會讓錯誤再發生一次！

Dennis: 我們可以再好好談一談嗎？

Jennifer: 滾出我的視線，你這個爛人！

Dennis: 所以，這是「不」的意思嗎？

字 單字及片語

類似的句子還有：
Let bygones be bygones.
(過去的就過去了。)

make up	v.和好
let's forgive and forget	過去的就原諒和遺忘吧
You've got me.	「被你說中了」的意思
patch up	v.平息紛爭
shackle(s)	n. 桎梏、枷鎖
ever happened to me	曾經發生在我身上
no way	不可能
calm down	v.冷靜下來
too...to	太...而不能
smack	v.啪一聲的甩、砸在...
talk it over	互相溝通、好好談談
Out of my sight	滾出我的視線

愛情實戰
unfaithful
不忠

CD 36

Kelly: I found out my husband was having an affair. I don't know what to do.

Dennis: Can you forgive him or have you lost all faith in your marriage?

Kelly: He's been fooling around for many years and I just can't take it anymore. He should live in Arab where polygamy is legal.

Dennis: Just listen to your heart and you will find a way out.

Kelly: Hmm. I just know marriage is about love, security and faith. One couldn't exist without the other. We'll try to work things out for the sake of our children, but I'll have to see what's in my best interest as well.

Dennis: I couldn't agree with you more.

對話譯點通

Kelly: 我發現我丈夫有外遇。我不知道該怎麼辦。

Dennis: 妳可以原諒他？還是妳已經失去對婚姻的信任呢？

Kelly: 他到處亂搞已經很多年了，我已經無法再忍受了。他應該住在阿拉伯，那裡一夫多妻是合法的。

Dennis: 就聽聽妳心裡的聲音吧！妳會找到出口的。

Kelly: 嗯。我只知道婚姻是愛、安全和信任，它們缺一不可的。為了我們小孩的緣故，我們會設法處理這件事，但是我同時也要知道，什麼是對我最有利的。

Dennis: 我非常同意。

 單字及片語

lose faith in	對某件事或人失去信任
faith	信任、信仰
fooling around = being unfaithful	不忠
polygamy	一夫多妻
bear	v.忍受
security	安全 = safety
	安全感 sense of safety
couldn't agree more	就字面翻成「我無法更同意了」意指，我相當同意。

例句：She's been messing around.
(她到處亂來。)
Messing around=being unfaithful

愛情實戰
differences of opinion
意見不合

 CD 37

Dennis: So, can I give you a goodnight kiss?

Amy: Sorry, I am not used to moving that fast. It's only our first date.

Dennis: Oh, I am sorry. I hope I didn't offend you.

Amy: It's ok. I heard about you foreigners!

Dennis: Hey!

Amy: Just kidding! Anyway, you have my phone number, right?

Dennis: Yeah, and you have mine too, right?

Amy: Well! Yes, but according to Chinese tradition and custom, we prefer to be called first.

Dennis: Yeah, I heard about you Chinese too!

Amy: Hey!!

對話譯點通

Dennis: 那麼，我可以給妳一個晚安吻嗎？
Amy: 抱歉！我不習慣進展地那麼快，這只是我們的第一次約會。
Dennis: 喔！我很抱歉。我希望我沒有冒犯妳才好。
Amy: 喔！沒關係。我早就聽說你們外國人囉！
Dennis: 嘿！
Amy: 開個玩笑啦！反正你有我的電話對吧！
Dennis: 嗯！妳也有我的，對吧？！
Amy: 嗯！但是根據中國人的傳統和禮俗，我們比較喜歡先通通電話。
Dennis: 嗯！我也早聽說你們中國人囉！！
Amy: 嘿！！

 單字及片語

goodnight kiss	晚安吻
be used to	習慣於
offend	v.冒犯
heard about	聽說、耳聞
foreigner	n.外國人
just kidding	開開玩笑
according to	根據
tradition	n.傳統
custom	n禮俗
prefer	v.較喜歡

愛情實戰
break up
分手

CD 38

Yvonne: I decided to break up with Tim.

Dennis: What's wrong? Are you ok?

Yvonne: The thing is I have always wanted to have a baby but he doesn't. I am tired of sleeping together and not officially together, you know what I mean?

Dennis: You mean he doesn't want to get married?

Yvonne: Yes, we are in completely different places and he thinks I am trying to tie him down for wanting a baby.

Dennis: Marriage is about commitments, and every person will be on a different schedule. Unless you both have the same timeline, then it's going to take a lot of hard work to get there.

Yvonne: Anyway, I have made up my mind and he owes me nothing in return.

Dennis: I think you have made the right decision. Anyway, welcome back to our singles club.

譯 對話譯點通

Yvonne: 我決定和 Tim 分手了。

Dennis: 怎麼了？妳還好吧？！

Yvonne: 主要是我一直想要一個小孩但是他不肯。我厭倦那種睡在一起，但不是「真正的」在一起。你知道我的意思嗎？

Dennis: 妳的意思是，他不想結婚？

Yvonne: 對。我們的立場完全不同，他認為想要小孩的我，只是為了想綁住他！

Dennis: 婚姻是種承諾，每一個人的時間表不太一樣。除非你們兩人剛巧都想結婚，不然會比較費力才可能走到那。

Yvonne: 總而言之，我已經下定決心，他也不欠我什麼。

Dennis: 我認為妳做了一個正確的決定。總之，歡迎回到我們的單身俱樂部。

字 單字及片語

decide to	v.決定去做什麼事
break up	v.分手、分離、崩潰的意思
What's wrong?	「怎麼了？」的意思
be tired of	v.對什麼感到厭倦
officially	adv.職務上的、官方的、正式的
be in different places	立場不同
commitment	n.承諾
make up my mind	下定決心
owe (某人) in return	不虧欠誰
make the right decision	做對決定
welcome back	歡迎回到...

what's wrong? = what's up? = what's going on? = is there something wrong？ 都是探問別人，「怎麼了？」的意思

of 是介係詞，後頭需加名詞或動名詞

(反義) change one's mind
改變某人的心意

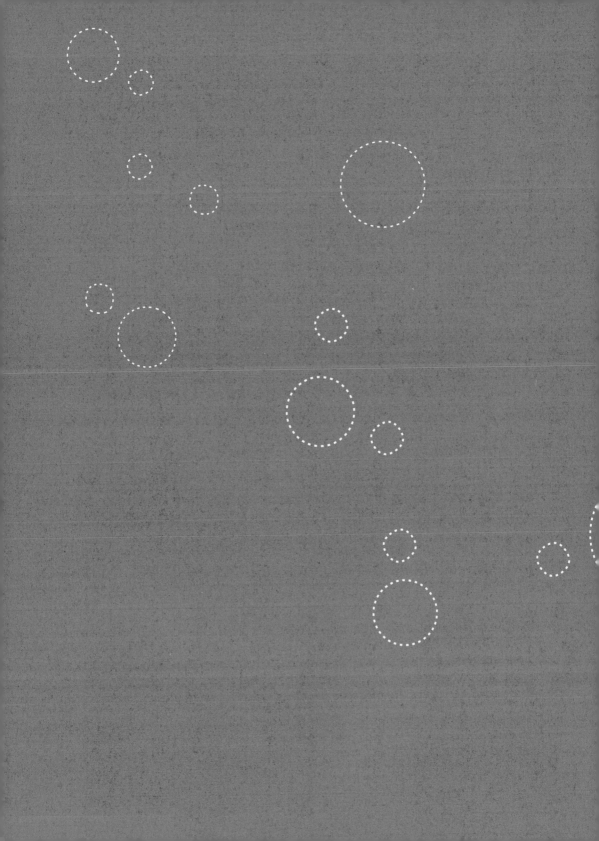

舊情人

我談的那場戀愛 . . .

　　我向來是個不後悔的人，一直都秉持著「向前走、不回頭」的人生態度。但是，在感情世界裡，也總難避免的去回想：自己是否曾經在某次的感情經驗裡，錯過了什麼？例如：鑽石或珍珠？再直接一點的說：如果命運讓我和舊情人在不經意的時刻重逢，像顆寶石的舊情人（或許最初它只是顆鵝卵石），比昔日更耀眼奪目，那我又會如何？又該如何？

　　幾日前，我遇到了這樣難得的經驗。那是在一次飛行的旅途，恰巧，我們都坐在同樣的商務艙，當時我記不得也認不出她，只在心裡面訝異：對座的女子，有種令人驚豔的氣質！當然，她很快注意到我眼神的善意。目光一交接，我很快想起了與她的過往，原來是我的舊情人！

　　我們很快地聊起來，記憶中的親切感和熟悉感，很神奇地回到我們身邊，雖然時空不同，大家也經歷了不同事情，但是好像當時相戀的化學作用，仍未流失。

　　那次巧遇後，我們互留了電話，似乎確認了彼此還有那麼些許的化學反應。下了飛機，各自回到現實。沒想到，幾個星期後，我們竟然又在高爾夫球場碰面。

　　好像電影裡的情節一樣。大家知道高爾夫球場，算是很紳士淑女運動的高雅空間，當天，她散發了最優雅的淑女氣質，當她進入我的眼簾，哇！我再無法分神了。我在場邊看著我的昔日戀人，她揮杆的姿態、修長曼妙的身型，舉手投足間，世界彷彿變得安靜而緩慢......終於，她看見我。

　　那天高球場的賽事結束後，有一場晚宴。我們各自換上最正式的晚禮服，我身著燕尾服，她穿上一襲鏤空的紫藍色晚禮服，真是耀眼逼人...，在那幾百人的場合裡，好幾次我們眼神交會，彷彿那一刻，眼中只有彼此，彷彿又回到熱戀中的愛侶，目光再無他人。

　　那晚我們都喝得有點醉，帶著一點微醺、一些悸動，兩人到室外聊天，好像很愉悅，又有一絲淡淡的悵惘，我哼起「The way we were」，往日情懷，一點點的惋惜，又有一點點為對方高興的心情。離開那裡之後，往事成雲煙，過往的對與錯，似乎也不再那麼重要了，我誠心祝福著老朋友，讓回憶停留在最美的瞬間。

 浪漫小語

The way we were

中文意思：我倆的過去，曾經是Barbara Streisand（芭芭拉·史翠珊）完美詮釋的一首經典名曲，中文歌名為「往日情懷」。動詞用were，是因為它發生在過去，如果能讓過往戀情，留下美好的回憶，是人生最美的事了。

懷念番外篇

聶雲分享經典情名曲

The way we were

Singer: Babara Streisand

The way we were （Lyrics）

Memories light the corners of my mind
回憶，照亮了我內心的角落

Misty water-colored memories of the way we were
那些朦朧如水彩般，我倆過去的回憶

Scattered pictures of the smiles we left behind
散落的照片，有我們遺落的笑容

Smiles we gave to one another for the way we were
我倆的過去給予彼此的笑容

Can it be that it was all so simple then
還能像從前一樣單純嗎？

Or has time rewritten every line
還有時間重寫每一行每一句嗎？

If we had the chance to do it all again
如果我們有機會重來一遍

Tell me, would we, could we
告訴我，可能嗎？可以嗎？

Memories may be beautiful and yet
回憶，也許仍然是美麗的

歌手：芭芭拉·史翠珊
往日情懷 (歌詞)

What's too painful to remember
那痛苦得讓我們不願想起的往事是什麼？

we simply choose to forget
我們乾脆選擇遺忘

So it's the laughter we will remember
我們將只記得歡笑

Whenever we remember the way we were
當我們回憶起我倆的過去

The way we were
我倆的過去

愛情實戰
old flame
舊情人

CD 39

Dennis: You will not believe who I ran into today!

Amy: Wow, you sound excited.

Dennis: I ran into my ex-girlfriend right in the middle of the street.

Amy: Great! What was it like?

Dennis: I couldn't believe it. It was like "Back To The Future", except it was really happening.

Amy: How did she look?

Dennis: Fine, but the thing is we were talking about the college days, it was a nice feeling and all the silly friends from school.

Amy: I meant is she still hot? Are you still attracted to her? Do you still have feeling for her? (Sounding upset)

Dennis: Honey, come on. I'm excited in a way of meeting up with an old friend. Old flames are a part of ancient history. You are the present, and you mean the world to me.

Amy: But you said she looked great.

Dennis: Yes, she looks great for a mother of two. I met her kids and her husband.

Amy: Oh! Sorry, wrong picture in mind.

譯 對話譯點通

Dennis: 你不會相信我今天遇到誰。

Amy: 哇,你的口氣聽起來很興奮。

Dennis: 就在街道上,我遇到我的前女友。

Amy: 是喔!感覺怎樣?

Dennis: 我不敢相信。有點像 "回到未來",它真的發生了。

Amy: 她看來如何?

Dennis: 不錯啊,我們談論起大學時候,曾經有過的美好回憶,還有那些傻的可愛的朋友。

Amy: 我的意思是,她還是很火辣嗎?你還是很被她吸引嗎?你對她還有感覺嗎?(聲音有些心煩)

Dennis: 親愛的,別這樣嘛!我只是遇到老朋友心裡開心。舊情人已經是古早歷史的一部份了。你是現在式,對我來說,你就是我的世界。

Amy: 但是你說她看起來很不錯。

Dennis: 是啊,對一個已經有兩個小孩的母親來說,她看起來是不錯啊。我還見了她孩子和她先生。

Amy: 喔!不好意思,我想錯了。

字 單字及片語

old flame	舊愛,口語化說法,通常很少用old lover。
run into	v.遇見,run的過去式ran
excited	adj.興奮的
be attracted to	受吸引
upset	adj.心煩的
ancient history	古早歷史
a mother of two	兩個小孩的媽
wrong picture in mind	想錯了

愛情實戰
refreshed memories
往日情懷

CD 40

(After running into her ex-boyfriend, Jason, Janet called her friend Dennis at 3am to pour her sorrows.)

Janet: Hey, are you asleep already?

Dennis: I was, but it's ok. What's up?

Janet: I ran into Jason tonight. I think I'm still a little emotional over the whole break up.

Dennis: You're calling me at 3am in the morning. I think it's more than a little emotional. Are you OK?

Janet: Hum, I don't know. He was just so stunning and vibrant. I think he is completely over me, but I'm still a mess.

Dennis: Come on! You have got to pull yourself together. You are a beautiful girl with a great sense of humor. I think anyone who can't see that doesn't deserve you.

Janet: Thanks. That's the nicest thing I've heard in a long time.

Dennis: What you need is to stop lingering on with those old memories and star making some new ones. You need to start meeting more new, fun, exciting and interesting people.

Janet: You're right. But where am I supposed to find a guy like that.

Dennis: I'm still up.

Janet: You're the best.

對話譯點通

（在和前男友**Jason**巧遇之後，**Janet**在半夜三點撥了通電話給他的朋友**Dennis**，傾訴她的悲傷）

Janet: 嘿！你睡著了嗎？

Dennis: 我本來在睡覺，但是沒關係，怎麼了？

Janet: 我今晚見著**Jason**了，我對我們已經徹底分手還是有點情緒。

Dennis: 妳凌晨三點打給我，我想不只是有點情緒而已，你還好吧？

Janet: 嗯，我不知道。他看起來如此動人又活躍。我覺得他完全忘記我了，我還是一灘爛泥。

Dennis: 別這樣。你必須把你自己振作起來，你既美麗又幽默，我想任何一個看不見你優點的人都配不上妳。

Janet: 謝謝。這是這段時間以來，我聽過最好的安慰。

Dennis: 你需要做的事，就是停止繼續徘徊在那些過去的記憶，開始創造新記憶。你該開始認識一些新的、好玩的、有活力的、有趣的人。

Janet: 你說的對。但我應該到哪發現那些人呢？

Dennis: 我還醒著。

Janet: 你真是太好了。

 單字及片語

asleep	adj. 睡著的
a little emotional	一點點情緒化的
break up	v. 分手
stunning	adj. 動人的
vibrant	adj. 活躍的
He is completely over me.	他完全忘記我
mess	n. 混亂
sense of humor	n. 幽默感
linger on	v. 徘徊、逗留
stop+Ving	v. 停止做某事
be supposed to	應該
I'm still up.	我還醒著
What's wake you up?	什麼吵醒你
wake you up	叫你起床

愛情實戰

second encounter
重逢

(Dennis bumped into his ex-girlfriend, Ann on the street and they started to chat.)

Dennis: Jesus, I almost didn't recognize you. You look great!

Ann: Thanks, you're not looking so bad yourself. What have you been up to?

Dennis: I just got back from a business trip yesterday, and I'm on my way to another meeting.

Ann: Quite busy?

Dennis: Just trying to make ends meet. You know, I never had a chance to tell you but I never meant to upset you like that. You meant everything to me, and I would never do anything that might jeopardize our relationship.

Ann: You know I don't even remember what made me so upset in the first place. But I do remember, you were quite a kisser.

Dennis: What a coincidence I have a crisp clear memory of that too.

Ann: Would you like to refresh or better yet relive those memories?

Dennis: Interesting suggestion, I think we deserve a second shot. I really don't think we should have broken up in the first place.

Ann: Yes, but this getting back together adds a little more drama to life don't you think?

對話譯點通

譯 對話譯點通

（**Dennis** 在街上偶遇他的前女友**Ann**，他們開始閒聊起來）

Dennis: 老天，我幾乎不認識你了。你看起來好棒！

Ann: 謝謝，你看起來也不錯。最近過得如何？

Dennis: 我昨天才出差回來，我正要去開一個會。

Ann: 相當忙喔？

Dennis: 只是勉強糊口混飯吃。你知道，我以前從來沒有機會告訴你，我從未想過用那種方式惹你生氣。對我來說你是一切，我不會做任何可能危及我們關係的事情。

Ann: 你知道我已經不記得，最初是什麼事情讓我生氣了。但是我確實記得，你是個接吻高手。

Dennis: 多巧啊我對這也有清晰的記憶。

Ann: 你想要重新回味或讓這些記憶更美好嗎？

Dennis: 真有趣的建議，我想我們值得再重新來一次，我真的不認為我們當初應該分手。

Ann: 對啊，但是這次復合，好像多加了些戲劇性，你不覺得嗎？

字 單字及片語

bump into	v.碰到
recognize	v.認識
What have you been up to?	近來如何
get back from	v.從（某地）回來
business trip	n.差旅
on my way	adv.往（某地）的路上
Just trying to make ends meet.	只是勉強混口飯吃
jeopardize	v.危及
in the first place	最初=in the beginning
coincidence	n.巧合
drama	n.戲劇
crisp	adj.鮮嫩的

還可以這樣說：
How's it going?
What's going on?
How have you been?

例句：
I am on my way home.
我正在回家的路上
I am on my way to the coffee shop.
我正在往咖啡館的路上

愛情實戰
How've you been?
別來無恙

(Dennis runs into his ex-girlfriend Jessica after their relationship fell apart three years ago.)

Dennis: Hey, Jessica, it's been forever! How have you been?

Jessica: You know, same old same old. I didn't except to run into you here. How have you been?

Dennis: Just going with the flow.

Jessica: Anyone special in you life?

Dennis: Can't say I found that someone yet. Still bumping from one relationship to another.

Jessica: Still afraid of a commitment I see.

Dennis: Yeah, I know. But Jessica, I must be honest with you. After all these years I really think you and I had something special. Sometimes I really think you are the one for me.

Jessica: Sorry, too little and too late.

Dennis: I hope I didn't break your heart then.

Jessica: I got over it. But I do think you still owe me some money.

Dennis: Nice seeing you again. Gotta run!

對話譯點通

（在和女友分手三年之後，Dennis巧遇Jessica了）

Dennis: 嘿，Jessica，真是好久不見，你都好嗎？

Jessica: 你知道的，還是老樣子，沒想到會遇見妳，你呢？

Dennis: 就是順其自然。

Jessica: 有遇到什麼特別的人嗎？

Dennis: 還沒遇到，感情的路還是跌跌撞撞。

Jessica: 我想你還是怕承諾。

Dennis: 是啊，我知道。但是Jessica，我得老實的跟你說，這麼多
年以來，我真的認為我和你有很特別的東西。有時候我真的
認為你是我的唯一。

Jessica: 抱歉，做得太少，時間太遲了。

Dennis: 我希望我那時沒有傷你的心。

Jessica: 我已經讓那些過去了，但是你好像還欠我錢。

Dennis: 很高興見到你，我得溜了。

 單字及片語

fall apart	v.關係結束，fall的過去式fell
It's been forever.	真是好久不見了！
run into	巧遇=bump into
Just going with the flow	就是順其自然
same old same old	老樣子，合在一起唸samo。
commitment	n.承諾
too little and too late	太少太遲
break your heart	傷你的心
I got over it.	我已經讓那些過去了
gotta	got to連在一起的說法。
	如：wanna = want to。

愛情實戰

lovesick
單相思

CD 43

(Dennis is chatting with his friend, Lucy, about his relationship problems)

Lucy: I really think you should get out more and meet some new friends.

Dennis: I don't know if I'm ready for that yet. I miss Cindy so much, and I think she is still hesitant to even answer my phone calls.

Lucy: Maybe you should try sending her flowers again.

Dennis: I did and she sent them back.

Lucy: Chocolates?

Dennis: Returned.

Lucy: She wouldn't answer your phone calls, but how about going over to her house and talking to her in person.

Dennis: Been there and done that. She said she'll call the police next time if I harass her again.

Lucy: Well maybe it's time you woke up and smell the coffee. In my opinion it's pretty much over.

Dennis: But I love her.

Lucy: Get a life!

譯 對話譯點通

（**Dennis**正在跟他朋友**Lucy**談他的感情困擾）

Lucy: 我真的覺得你應該多出去走走，認識一些新的朋友。

Dennis: 我不知道我是否準備好了。我好想念Cindy，而且我想她仍然在猶豫是否回我電話。

Lucy: 也許你應該再送她一些花。

Dennis: 我有啊不過她送還回來了。

Lucy: 巧克力呢？

Dennis: 也送回來了。

Lucy: 她不回你電話，那如果去她住處，當面跟她說呢？

Dennis: 我已經去那裡做你所說的，她說如果下次我再騷擾她，她會打電話報警。

Lucy: 喔，好吧，也許這是你該醒過來，聞聞咖啡香的時候了！在我看來，差不多是沒得玩了。

Dennis: 但是我愛她。

Lucy: 你太遜了！

字 單字及片語

chat with	v.談天
get out more	多出去走走
hesitant	v.猶豫
return	v.送還
in person	當面
harass	v.騷擾
wake up	v.清醒
in my opinion	我的想法
get a life	太遜了

老外注重生活，認為生活中除了工作愛情以外，還有其他如家庭、運動等重要的事，當他們看見某個人的生活過得乏味貧瘠，就常會說：**Get a life!** 意味著對方太遜了，應該好好面對生活。

愛情實戰

sticking around
藕斷絲連

 CD 44

> **Dennis** 小提醒：
> **Break up** 是指男女朋友之間分手，沒有誰拋棄誰的意思。如果你要強調誰拋棄誰，可以使用**dump**這個字。**Dump trash** 就是倒垃圾的意思。
> 有時分手也可以用**end our relationship** 表示。例如：**I have decided to end our relationship.** 我已經決定結束這段感情。

Yvonne: My ex-boyfriend called me last night to tell me about his recent break up.

Dennis: What did you say?

Yvonne: What can I say? I just tried to pamper him a little.

Dennis: You are such a softy. He was the one that dumped you in the first place.

Yvonne: I know. But I just can't bring myself to hate him.

Dennis: So what? Are you thinking about getting back together with him?

Yvonne: Not gonna happen! I just happened to think of the old saying "Men's love are deeper but don't last as long; Women's love are longer but not as deep."

Dennis: Too bad this saying is only for relationships and not their sexual ability ,you know, "Longer and deeper"

Yvonne: That's gross, please get your mind out of the gutter!

Dennis: Just kidding.

（譯） 對話譯點通

Yvonne: 我的前男友昨晚打電話給我,說他最近的分手。

Dennis: 那你怎麼說?

Yvonne: 我能怎麼說呢?我就試著去呵護他些。

Dennis: 你心腸太好了啦!當初是他甩了妳。

Yvonne: 我知道。但是我就是沒辦法恨他。

Dennis: 那又怎樣?你想跟他復合嗎?

Yvonne: 不可能!我只是剛剛想到一句古老的諺語:「男人的愛情深而不久,而女人的感情則久而不深。」

Dennis: 真可惜,這句諺語只是用在男女情感而不是在講性能力:持久而深。

Yvonne: 真噁心,請停止你的骯髒念頭。

Dennis: 只是開玩笑啦!

（字） 單字及片語

recent	adj.最近的
pamper	v.寵、放縱
softy	n.心腸好,柔軟
dump	v.倒(垃圾)、拋棄(感情)
so what	那又怎樣呢
Not gonna happen!	不可能,gonna=going to
slang	n.諺語
That's gross.	真噁心
gutter	n.排水溝
get your mind out of the gutter	停止你的髒念頭

還可以這樣説:
It really grossed me out.
feel like vomiting
feel nauseated
feel sick
feel disgusting

愛情實戰
dilemma
進退兩難

 CD 45

Stacy: It's so hard to find the perfect guy out there.

Dennis: Stacy can't find a man? That's a first.

Stacy: It's not about finding a man but the good ones. You know there's a saying "Men are like parking spaces, all the good ones are taken and the ones that are left are too small or handicapped. "

Dennis: There's got to be some nice candidates in your life right now.

Stacy: The ones that are well established are either too old, too boring, or have no idea how to have a good time at all. But all the cute and interesting ones are always the ones that are too poor to afford my life style.

Dennis: What does your intuition tell you?

Stacy: Go out with the rich ones during the day and party with the cute ones at night.

Dennis: Good idea, but you are so bad.

譯 對話譯點通

Stacy: 要發現一個好的男人真難。

Dennis: Stacy 找不到男人，這真是頭一遭。

Stacy: 無關找不找的到，而是好不好。你知道有句俗話，男人就像停車格，所有好的早就被佔了，剩下的不是太小就是有點缺陷。

Dennis: 你現在的生活中，應該有些候選人吧！

Stacy: 那些有經濟能力的不是太老，就是太無聊，不然就是對於享受生活毫無概念。但是那些可愛的、有趣的，總是窮的不足以負擔我的生活方式。

Dennis: 那你的直覺怎麼說？

Stacy: 白天跟有錢的一起出去，晚上跟可愛的在一起玩樂。

Dennis: 好主意，但你這樣真的很壞。

字 單字及片語

That's a first.	這是頭一回
There's a saying.	有句俗語
parking spaces	停車格
handicapped	adj.有缺陷的
handicap	n.障礙
candidate	n.候選人
well established	adj.有錢有勢的，有社會地位、有影響力的
not at all	一點也不
afford	v.負擔、提供
too poor to afford	太窮而不能負擔，too...to，太...而不能
intuition	n.直覺

愛情實戰
sex with an ex
和舊情人發生性關係

Karen: My ex is moving to Paris.

Dennis: Hence, it's your "ex" right? That means it's in the past tense, which shouldn't mean anything to you anymore.

Karen: Well, the sex with him was great!

Dennis: Point taken, but emphasize on the word "was"?

Karen: Well, and "is" still great.

Dennis: You mean you two are still sleeping together?

Karen: Only occasionally.

Dennis: You're playing with fire. What if your present boyfriend finds out?

Karen: I know, but it was so fun. I guess I wouldn't see him anymore.

Dennis: That's the right attitude.

Karen: Unless I go to Paris for my business trip next week, then we just might meet and catch up.

Dennis: Catch up on what, sex? You are terrible, but make sure you tell me all the juicy details when you come back.

對話譯點通

Karen: 我的前男友要搬回巴黎了。

Dennis: 注意，"前"男友，對嗎？那意味著那段感情已經是過去式了，對你不在有意義了。

Karen: 嗯，以前跟他的性生活真的很讚！

Dennis: 收到，你強調的重點是"以前"？

Karen: 嗯，現在其實還是很好。

Dennis: 你的意思是，你們現在還是一起炒飯？

Karen: 偶爾啦。

Dennis: 你在玩火啦，如果你現在男友發現會怎樣？

Karen: 我知道，但是這真的很有趣。我想我不會再看到他了。

Dennis: 這才是對的態度嘛。

Karen: 除非下週我去巴黎出差，到時我們可能見個面，剛好趕上。

Dennis: 剛好趕上什麼？嘿咻？你真的很恐怖，確定你回來後會告訴我刺激的精采情節。

 單字及片語

ex	前任
hence	adv.提示、註解，表示"注意囉！"的意思
in the past tense	過去式
point taken	收到
emphasize	v.強調
occasionally	adv.偶爾
You're playing with fire.	你在玩火
find out	v.發現
catch up	v.趕上
terrible	adj.可怕的
juicy details	刺激的細節，非常口語化的說法

愛情實戰

that cute ex
可愛的舊情人

CD 47

Cynthia: Do you ever think about your ex?

Dennis: Sometimes.

Cynthia: I can't get my ex-boyfriend out of my mind and it's driving me nuts.

Dennis: Well, we all thought you were going to tie the knot with that one. He's a great looking dude.

Cynthia: Yeah, I don't know why I let him go. I miss him all the time.

Dennis: I remember why you let him go, he was so good looking that anywhere you went, girls were always coming on to him and it drove you bananas.

Cynthia: I miss him so much.

Dennis: Forget him. Find someone who won't give you a heart attack every time you go out together.

Cynthia: Should I call him?

Dennis: To do what? Beg! Save the embarrassment.

譯 對話譯點通

Cynthia: 你曾經想過你的前任女友嗎？

Dennis: 有時候會吧。

Cynthia: 我不能忘記我的前男友，這簡直快讓我抓狂了。

Dennis: 嗯，我們原以為你和他會走入婚姻，那老兄是個大帥哥哩。

Cynthia: 是啊，我不知道為何會讓他離開，我常常想起他。

Dennis: 我記得你會何讓他離開ㄟ，他長得太帥，你們到哪，女孩總想法接近他，這讓你快抓狂了。

Cynthia: 我好想他。

Dennis: 忘了他吧，去找個人，不會在你們每次出去時，都讓你心臟病發。

Cynthia: 我應該打電話給他嗎？

Dennis: 打去幹嘛？乞求愛情？保留點顏面啦。

 字 單字及片語

還可以這樣說：
drive me crazy
It drives me bananas.

drive me nuts	把我逼瘋了，讓人抓狂。
think	v.認為，I thought 我原以為
tie the knot	結為連理，意思指結婚
great looking	長得好看
dude	n.老兄、花花公子（俚語）
Save the embarrassment.	保留顏面

愛情實戰
friendship between the opposite sex
異性間的友誼

CD 48

(Dennis is talking to his friend, Alisa)

Alisa: Dave tried to kiss me yesterday.

Dennis: That dog.

Alisa: I was shocked, too. I mean, we were such good friends and he had to go and pull a stunt like that.

Dennis: How could he?

Alisa: I mean, I trusted him. And now it will be so weird when I see him again.

Dennis: Well, you can't really blame him. After all, you are a very attractive woman.

Alisa: That's not the point. We were just friends and nothing more.

Dennis: But guys don't work like that. We get confused easily with the girls.

Alisa: Why?

Dennis: You see, sometimes guys think with our big head which for the most part will keep us out of trouble. But sometimes our little head takes over and we get into situations we don't even know how to get out of.

Alisa: So when you said I was an attractive woman, was that your big head talking or your little head.

Dennis: I'll answer with my big head and tell you, I will keep that to myself.

譯 對話譯點通

（**Dennis** 正在跟他的朋友**Alisa** 談天。）

Alisa: Dave 昨天想吻我。

Dennis: 那畜牲。

Alisa: 我也很訝異。我是說，我們是如此好的朋友，而他竟然出現這種驚人之舉。

Dennis: 他怎麼能這樣做。

Alisa: 我的意思是，我信任他，但是現在我看見他，感覺就怪怪的。

Dennis: 嗯，你不能真的怪他啦，畢竟，你是一個如此吸引人的女子。

Alisa: 這不是重點，我們只是朋友而已。

Dennis: 但是男生不會這樣想喔。跟女孩子一起，我們常很容易迷惘。

Alisa: 為什麼？

Dennis: 你要了解，大部分時候我們用大頭思考，這避免讓我們惹上麻煩，但有時候小頭掌控了一切，這會讓我們麻煩到無法脫身。

Alisa: 所以，當你說我是一個很具吸引力的女人，這是出自你的大頭還是小頭。

Dennis: 我會用我的大頭思考然後告訴你，我會保留這個答案。

字 單字及片語

stunt	n.引人注目的事
pull a stunt	做出驚人之舉
How could he?	他怎麼這樣
blame	v.責備
That's not the point.	那不是重點
Guys don't work like that.	男生不這樣想
get confused	v.混淆、迷惑
out of trouble	遠離麻煩
take over	v.佔領
get out	脫身
keep that to myself	保留給自己

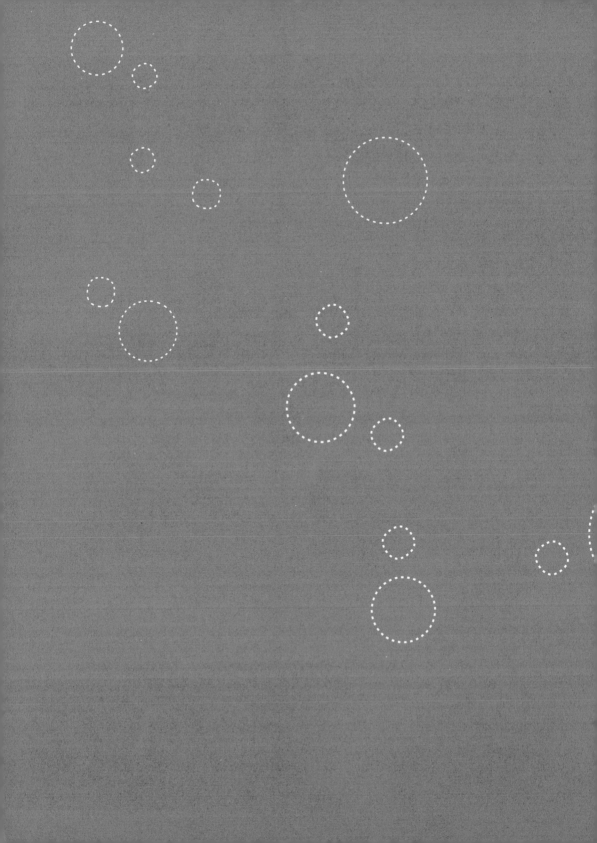

修成正果

我談的那場戀愛...

我想所有的女人都很可愛，只是如果要找結婚對象，可能不只需要可愛，還得要有些別的，例如：外型、個性、能力、或者別的，跟個人需求有關。交往的過程，其實就等於一個長期的面試，如果出現的問題可以持續的被解答，那麼走入婚姻的可能性也就大了。

以我的經驗來說，「安靜和沈默」是我在兩人關係中追求的一件事。那是一種不需要說話，也可以感覺舒服的絕佳默契，簡簡單單的依偎，其實也就是一種幸福了！

有人說：「Love is enjoyment；Marriage is tolerance.」（愛情是享受，婚姻是忍受。）或許真的是也不一定，怎麼說呢，走入婚姻會得到一些，也總會失去一些，但是我要說的是，有些難能可貴的幸福，只有真正落實在婚姻生活當中，你才有可能會發現。

婚姻是一種非常貼近現實的賭注，有人敢下注，你敢不敢做莊？我從不後悔自己做出結婚的承諾。

我還記得那個美好的夜晚，我老婆Judy點頭，願意和我一起攜手走下半生。那晚，我激動著，幾乎無法睡著。

　　那晚，我想起我們曾經一起散步。那是微涼的夏夜，我們走在公園，前面剛好有一棵樹，我說我要抬腳踢到樹枝，她笑我不可能，我真的踢到了，換她來試，她說，這樣做好蠢！說完，她踢腿，想踢到樹枝，踢不到，我幫她，我手撐著她，她賣力踢，還是踢不到，最後終於踢到了，我們笑倒在地上，已經累的喘不過氣⋯⋯

　　對我來說，那瞬間的體會，就是永恆的幸福。我和Judy單純的從小孩子的天真，一路玩耍，然後，一起走進兩人親密的婚姻世界裡。

 浪漫小語

Love is enjoyment ; Marriage is tolerance.

「愛情是享受，婚姻是忍受。」這句名言帶著幽默和諷刺。婚姻，是一個家庭的完成，讓我們的生命邁向另一層次，或許沒想像中完美，或許沒戀愛般甜蜜，但有一天你會發現，能夠與一個伴侶和一個承諾，安穩地相擁入眠，會是件滿足的事！

愛情實戰
get back together
復合

Dennis: What's up, Jamie? You seem puzzled.

Jamie: You are not going to believe what happened today. My ex called and wants to get back together.

Dennis: And what did you say?

Jamie: I need some time to think this through. I don't want to be back where we were.

Dennis: And where might that be?

Jamie: Well he's always tied up with work, or friends and it just seems that I am never a part of his priority list.

Dennis: Sounds reasonable. But does he love you?

Jamie: Well, he says he does and he wishes for a second chance.

Dennis: And you still have feelings for him, don't you?

Jamie: I do, and that's why this is killing me. What am I gonna do?

Dennis: It's sounds like you already know. If you love him, work it out. Don't let true love slip away.

對話譯點通

Dennis:	怎麼啦？Jamie？妳看起來似乎有心事？
Jamie:	你不會相信今天發生了什麼事情。我前男友打電話給我要求復合。
Dennis:	那妳怎麼說？
Jamie:	我需要時間想想。我害怕又犯同樣的錯誤。
Dennis:	像是什麼？
Jamie:	嗯，他總是以工作、或是朋友為優先，似乎我總不在他的優先名單中。
Dennis:	聽起來合情合理。但是他愛你嗎？
Jamie:	嗯，他說是啊，他希望再有一次機會。
Dennis:	妳對他還有感覺，不是嗎？
Jamie:	沒錯，就是這樣我才這麼痛苦，我該怎麼做呢？
Dennis:	聽起來妳已經知道怎麼做了啊，假如你愛他，就設法去解決問題吧，不要讓真愛溜走。

單字及片語

You seem puzzled.	你看來有心事
I don't want to be back where we were.	不想我們重蹈覆轍
tie up	v.繫住；綁住
priority	n.優先
priority list	n.優先排序
reasonable	adj.合情合理的
wish for + N	希望
work out	ph.想法解決
slip away	v.溜走

愛情實戰
go steady
穩定交往

CD 50

(Janis is chatting with her friend, Dennis, about her boyfriend, Robbie)

Janis Robbie popped the big question last night.

Dennis That's great! Tell me all about it!

Janis: That's not the point. The point is I don't know if he's the one.

Dennis: Why not?

Janis: He's 30 years old and still living with his parents, he just seems like a big boy sometimes.

Dennis: Does he love you?

Janis: Yes, but sometimes I don't know if he loves me because I'm his girlfriend or because I take care of him like his mother.

Dennis: All guys are like babies sometimes. Don't worry, they all grow up eventually.

Janis: And if not?

Dennis: Then just love that big over grown baby. Just as long as he loves you right back.

譯 對話譯點通

（Janis 正在跟他的朋友Dennis談她的男友，Robbie）

Janis: Robbie 昨晚問了那個問題。（意指求婚）

Dennis: 哇！真好，快告訴我細節。

Janis: 這不是重點，重點是我不確定他是不是我生命中的那個人。

Dennis: 為何？

Janis: 他已經三十歲了，但是還住在父母家裡，我不知道，有時候他像個大男孩。

Dennis: 他愛你嗎？

Janis: 他愛，但有時候我會疑惑，他愛我是因為我是他女友，還是因為我像他媽一樣照顧他。

Dennis: 有時候，男人就像嬰兒，不用擔心，最後總會長大。

Janis: 要是沒有呢？

Dennis: 那就繼續愛這個超大嬰兒，只要他也愛你。

字 單字及片語

pop	v.突然提問
pop the question	突然提出問題
Why not?	為什麼不
take care of	照顧
eventually	adv.最後、終於
as long as	只要

你要買這本書嗎？幹麻不買！
Would you like to buy the book?Why not?
我已經有一本了。
I already have one.

愛情實戰

propose
求婚

CD 51

Julia: Joe finally proposed to me last week, I was so thrilled.

Dennis: That's wonderful. I want to know all about it.

Julia: Well, he took me to that little deli we went to on our first date and halfway through dinner he got down on one knee and popped the question.

Dennis: That is so sweet. I didn't know he had it in him.

Julia: I have a favor to ask you, will you be my best man?

Dennis: Sure, I'd love to. When is the wedding?

Julia: Well, we haven't decided yet. I can't believe I am finally getting married!

Dennis Look at you!I have never seen you so happy. Are you going to have a bachelor's party?

Julia: I don't know.

Dennis: Where do you plan to have this wedding?

Julia: I don't know?

Dennis: And the guest list?

Julia: Oh no, I have no idea yet. There is so much to be done. How am I going to handle all of this?

Dennis Don't worry, just take it one step at a time.

Julia: You're right, that's what best friends are for, or should I say that's what the best man is for.

譯 對話譯點通

Julia:　Joe上週向我求婚了，我真樂透了。

Dennis:　真棒耶！告訴我所有細節！

Julia:　好吧，他帶我去我們第一次約會的店，晚餐吃到一半，他一膝跪下，提出求婚。

Dennis:　真甜蜜。我不知道他還有這一面。

Julia:　我有件事想請你幫忙，你願意當我的男儐相嗎？

Dennis:　當然，我很樂意。婚禮什麼時候舉行？

Julia:　嗯，我們還沒有決定。我不敢相信我終於要結婚了。

Dennis:　看看你。我從沒見你這樣開心。你們準備辦一個告別單身派對嗎？

Julia:　我不知道。

Dennis:　婚禮準備在哪裡舉行呢？

Julia:　我不知道。

Dennis:　宴客名單呢？

Julia:　喔！完了，我毫無概念。有好多事情要準備，我一個人怎麼可能忙的過來？

Dennis:　不用擔心，一步一步來。

Julia:　你説的對，好朋友是用來幹嘛的，或者我該説，男儐相是用來幹嘛的。

 字 單字及片語

propose	妳看來有心事	例句：Josh proposed. （Josh求婚了）
propose marriage to me	向我求婚	
	也可以直接説propose	
thrilled	adj.相當高興、興奮	
deli	n.熟食店	
halfway	半途中	
best man	n.伴郎、男儐相	
look at you	看看你、瞧瞧你	
bachelor	n.單身漢	
bachelor's party	n.單身派對	
handle	v.處理	

愛情實戰
meeting the parents
拜見雙親

(Dennis is asking her girlfriend Lisa to meet his parents.)

Dennis: My parents are coming to town tomorrow, would you like to meet them?

Lisa: yes, I mean no, I mean I don't know.

Dennis: Come on, what's wrong? You guys will love each other.

Lisa: But meeting the parents seems like such a big deal. I don't know if I'm ready for that yet. I mean we have only been seeing each other for a few months.

Dennis: Hey, the past few months have been wonderful. I want you to not only meet my parents, but I want you to meet my entire, big and embarrassing family. Including all my weird cousins.

Lisa: You know what? I would love to. But just a fair warning, I have some freaky relatives in my family too.

Dennis: Great, it looks like we were made for each other.

對話譯點通

（Dennis 希望女友 Lisa 可以見見他的父母）

Dennis: 我父母親明天要來城裡，我希望妳能見見他們。
Lisa: 好，不，我的意思是我不知道。
Dennis: 別這樣，怎麼了？你們會喜歡彼此的。
Lisa: 但是見父母親是這樣大的事，我不知道我是否準備好了。我的意思是，我們才認識幾個月。
Dennis: 嘿，是很棒的幾個月，我不只希望你認識我的父母，我希望你認識我全部的親戚、還有尷尬的令人難為情的大家族，包括我那些怪怪的堂兄弟表姊妹。
Lisa: 你知道嗎？我很願意。但我也得先提醒你，我的家族中也有一些怪怪的親戚。
Dennis: 這樣正好，看來我們真是天生一對。

 單字及片語

What's wrong?	怎麼了
you guys	你們，非常口語的説法
entire	adj.全部的
embarrassing	adj.令人難為情的
weird	adj.怪怪的
	類似的説法還有：freaky
cousin	n.(堂/表)兄弟姊妹
just a fair warning	誠實的忠告，fair有平等的、誠實的意思。
relative	n.親戚
We were made for each other.	我們真是天生一對

祝福番外篇

聶雲心法傳授

讓戀情贏得祝福！

　　有人說，不被親人祝福的婚姻很難幸福。我沒遭遇過，所以無法判斷。但是，我可以告訴你，擁有親人的祝福是件相當幸福的事，如果還在談戀愛階段，親人的祝福會使戀情加溫，並且容易達陣，運氣好的話，他們可以成為忠實戰友。所以，首先，要試圖拉攏他們，讓他們成為你的軍師。

怎樣贏得祝福呢？

　　首先，「生日不可忘，禮物不能少」，和情人「Go steady」（穩定交往）之後，可以提出拜訪對方父母的想法，除了讓對方知道，你對長輩的尊重外，也有助於儘早了解對方的家庭，並且讓對方知道你在認真經營這段感情。然後，要細心的記下家長的生日，展現貼心與忠誠。這不是心機手段喔，這是一種身為晚輩的懂事與體貼（當然也是一種收買的技巧啦！）（笑）

　　然後，要「事必躬親，時時探問」，就算戀情穩定發展，也不代表革命成功，為了避免功虧一簣，還是要持續巴結，用力籠絡。生日或重要節日之外，很多事情需要你處理，就攬下來做好。當你把對方的事與煩惱當作自己的，已經表示了自己有能力承擔，也是負責任的人，父母長輩稱讚，這樣，距離達陣的目標也不遠了。

有人問我，收編對方親人成為自己的戰友，有什麼好處啊？好處當然很多，最基本的，就是佈眼線，防患未然啊。當然啦，每個家庭的狀況各有不同，親人之間的對待方式也不太一樣。前面提到的，主要是我自己個人的經驗，讓大家在感情經營上做參考，還是要祝福各位：戀情早日修成正果！

CD 53

愛情實戰

shotgun marriage
奉子成婚

Dennis 小提醒：
關於懷孕有幾種説法，例如：**They are expecting**.
（他們將有小孩了。）**She's with child. / There's a bun in the oven**. （懷孕了）俚語。

(Dennis asked his friend Lucy to see a movie this weekend, but Lucy isn't interested)

Lucy: Hey, I'm getting married!

Dennis: Wow, that's great, but that's kind of fast. You've only been dating Jim for a few months. What made you guys decided to do this?

Lucy: Well we didn't actually decide, we had help from someone else.

Dennis: What? His parents, right? You know that's what happens when you meet the elders. They must be in such a rush to see their son settle down with a nice girl like you.

Lucy: No, we had help from someone else and that someone would be around in another 9 months or so.

Dennis: Wow! Congratulations!

Lucy: Thanks, but I just hope he's marrying me because he loves me and not because he has to.

Dennis: Nonsense, you two are the cutest couple I know. You were made for each other.

Lucy: Yah, a shotgun wedding.I'm kind of excited and scared at the same time.

Dennis: Well, a shotgun wedding means we have to work fast. I don't think the bride should have the biggest belly that day.

Lucy: Oh, don't remind me.

譯 對話譯點通

（Dennis 邀他的朋友 Lucy 這週末去看場電影，但 Lucy 似乎不怎麼感興趣）

Lucy: 嘿，我要結婚了。

Dennis: 哇，真好，不過來的真突然。你才跟 Jim 約會幾個月吧，是什麼讓你們做出這樣的決定？

Lucy: 嗯，不完全是我們的決定，我們得到了某人的幫忙。

Dennis: 誰？他父母，對嗎？果然見過就會這樣子。他們一定急著看兒子和你這樣好的女孩穩定下來。

Lucy: 不，我們是因為其他人的幫忙，那人大概再九個月後會出現。所以…

Dennis: 哇！恭喜啊！

Lucy: 謝謝，但我希望他娶我是因為他愛我，而不是因為他有了小孩而不得不。

Dennis: 別胡思亂想，你們是我認識中最可愛的一對，你們是天造地設。

Lucy: 是啊，奉子成婚！我真是既驚又喜。

Dennis: 也是啦，奉子成婚就意味著我們動作得快一點，我想新娘那天不應該挺著大肚子。

Lucy: 喔，不要再提醒我了。

字 單字及片語

I'm getting married.	我要結婚了
kind of fast	有點快
help from someone else	得自別人的幫忙
around in another 9 months	大約再九個月，around，大約的意思。
congratulations	n.恭喜
nonsense	感嘆辭，胡說、胡亂想之意。
a shotgun wedding	n.奉子成婚，這裡做名詞用。
belly	n.肚子
remind	v.提醒

愛情實戰
inter-racial marriage
異國婚姻

 CD 54

(Dennis is talking to his American friend, Sarah, who wants to get married to a Taiwanese guy)

Sarah: Do you believe inter-racial relationships can work?

Dennis: Sure, why not. I mean it could be difficult with the cultural differences but it could also add some spice into life.

Sarah: I'm seeing a Taiwanese guy and it's getting a little serious. I think he wants to introduce me to his family. But I just don't know how they'll react to a white girlfriend.

Dennis: You have a great personality, everyone I know loves you. I don't think you have anything to worry about.

Sarah: Ya, you're right. I can handle this. It'll be a piece of cake.

Dennis: Let me just remind you that Taiwanese families can be pretty big sometimes.

Sarah: Got it.

Dennis: They can get kind of loud too.

Sarah: No problem.

Dennis: Oh, and they are very affectionate.

Sarah: You're making me nervous, maybe you can come with me and act as an icebreaker or something.

Dennis: He's not my boyfriend.

對話譯點通

（Dennis 跟美國友人 Sarah 聊天，她想嫁給一個台灣男子。）

Sarah: 你覺得異國婚姻行的通嗎？

Dennis: 當然行的通，為何行不通？我的意思是，也許因為文化不同會比較辛苦些，但是同時也會為生活增添許多趣味。

Sarah: 我目前跟一個台灣男生約會，感情進展到有些認真了。我想他想介紹我給他的家人認識，但是我不知道他們對我這外國白人女朋友會有什麼反應？

Dennis: 你有很好的性格，我認識的人都喜愛你，我想你不需要擔心。

Sarah: 是啊，你說的對。我可以應付的來，只不過是小事一椿！

Dennis: 只是我要提醒你，有些台灣人的家族非常龐大。

Sarah: 了解。

Dennis: 他們會有點吵雜大聲。

Sarah: 沒問題。

Dennis: 喔，還有，他們極度的熱情。

Sarah: 你讓我開始緊張了，也許你可以跟我一起去，幫我打破僵局或者其他什麼的。

Dennis: 他可不是我男朋友喔！

單字及片語

cultural differences	n.文化差異
spice	n.趣味、香料
add some spice	增添某些趣味
serious	adj.認真、嚴肅
introduce...to	v.介紹…給
react	v.反應
personality	n.性格
worry about	ph.擔心
a piece of cake	ph.小意思
affectionate	adj.是充滿深情的、溫柔親切的
icebreaker	n.打破僵局

愛情實戰

VOWS
誓言

Dennis 小提醒：
承諾有幾種講法：
I promise.（我保證）I give you my word.
／ I will keep my promise.／I will keep my
words. truse me.（相信我）Believe me.／You
can count on me.／You can take my word
for it. I won't let you down.（我不會讓你失望）
I will do my best.／I won't disappoint you.

Dennis: Are you ready our big day tomorrow?

Rosemary: Just go in and say "I do", I think I can handle that.

Dennis: No, we need to exchange vows and you have to come up with something original.

Rosemary: But I don't know what to say. Can I just let you say yours first and say I feel the exact same way?

Dennis: That is so cheesy.

Rosemary: Alright. I will come up with something. But promise you wouldn't laugh if it's too mushy.

Dennis: The mushier the better.

對話譯點通

Dennis:	明天是我們的大喜日子，你準備好了嗎？
Rosemary:	只要走進去，説：「我願意」，我想我可以做好的。
Dennis:	不是喔，我們需要交換誓言，而且你得講一些發自內心的感言。
Rosemary:	但我不知道要説什麼呢。我可以讓你先説你的，然後我說感受跟你一模一樣，這樣可以嗎？
Dennis:	這樣太遜了。
Rosemary:	好吧，我會準備想要説的話。但是如果我講的太肉麻，你要答應我不可以笑喔。
Dennis:	講得愈肉麻愈好啦。

 單字及片語

big day	重要日子
exchange vows	交換誓言
come up with	ph.想出
original	adj.原始的、有獨創性的、新穎的
feel the same way	感受相同
exact	adj.精確的
feel the exact same way	感受一模一樣
so cheesy	太遜了
alright	好吧
mushy	adj.肉麻的
The...+比較級adj ...the better	愈...愈好

> 例句：Everyone is so cheesy.
> (每個人都好遜)

> 例句：
> **The sooner the better .** (愈快愈好)

愛情實戰
like husband, like wife
夫妻臉

 CD 56

> **Dennis 小提醒：**
> 很多台灣人説夫妻臉，用 **couple face**，但是老美並不是這樣説喔，夫妻臉，如果一定要用英文表達，可以借用 **like father, like son**（有其父必有其子），説成 **like husband, like wife**。

(Alice is talking to her American friend, Dennis.)

Alice: Hey, is that your wife in the picture?

Dennis: Yup, happily married for 3 years.

Alice: Well, there's a Taiwanese expression called "couple faces", which means you guys look similar to each other, and definitely will get along very well!

Dennis: Wow! I guess in English we would call it "like husband, like wife".

Alice: Sounds great!

對話譯點通

（Alice 跟她的美國朋友 Dennis 聊天）

Alice: 嘿，照片中是你太太嗎？
Dennis: 對啊，我們已經美滿婚姻三年了。
Alice: 嗯，台灣有句話可以表達：夫妻臉。意思是說，你們看起來很
　　　　像，而且很合得來。
Dennis: 哇！我想，如果用英文說，就是：like husband，like wife.
Alice: 沒錯。

 單字及片語

expression	n.表達
similar	adj.相似的
similar to	與相像
definitely	adv.肯定地、明確地
get along very well	相處得很好

例句：
My opinions are similar to yours.
(我的看法與你相似)
His question is similar to yours.
(他的問題和你的相似)

愛情實戰
mistress
情婦

 CD 57

Dennis 小提醒：
除了**mistress**之外，**paramour**、**a lover on the side**都有情婦的意思。如果同時與許多異性交往，可以說「**play the field**」、外遇說「**an affair**」，不正常的戀愛關係，叫做「**a love affair**」。

Isabel: My boss wants me to have dinner with him again.

Dennis: Doesn't he have to go home to his wife?

Isabel: That's the thing. He keeps dumping his family problems to me. And I really don't know what to say to him.

Dennis: But dinner is all he wants right?

Isabel: Well, he's been trying to give me expensive gifts and I am really trying to keep my distance.

Dennis: Sounds like a dirty old man is looking for a mistress.

Isabel: So what you're saying is that he is trying to seduce me?

Dennis: What I'm saying is : stay the hell away from that pervert.

對話譯點通

Isabel: 我老闆又要我和他一起晚餐。
Dennis: 他難道不需要回家跟太太一起嗎？
Isabel: 就是啊，他一直把他家的問題丟給我。我真不知道該對他說什麼。
Dennis: 但只是晚餐，對嗎？
Isabel: 還有，他一直試著送我昂貴的禮物，我一直試著保持距離。
Dennis: 聽起來，像是一個老不休正在獵情婦。
Isabel: 你是說，他試圖在勾引我嗎？
Dennis: 我要說的是，遠離情婦那條不歸路，遠離那個變態。

 單字及片語

dump	v.丟
keep distance	保持距離
is looking for	正在尋找
seduce	v.勾引
Are you trying to seduce me?	你是在勾引我嗎？
stay the hell away	遠離地獄
pervert	n.變態

Seduce是指用言語或行為勾引某人。這句話在美國派（American pie）當中有出現過，劇中有個男生最後找不到舞會的伴了，結果跑去勾引一個老女人，女人就說了：Are you trying to seduce me？

愛情實戰

extramarital relationship
婚外情

Selina: I'm seeing someone from work.

Dennis: Does your husband know?

Selina: Are you kidding?

Dennis: How did this happen?

Selina: Well it was the Christmas party and we ran into each other in the meeting room, and he was just so cute in his Santa uniform and....

Dennis: I meant how could you let something like this happen. Your are a married woman.

Selina: I know but I am just a woman.

Dennis: You are walking on thin ice! Your husband will kill you if he finds out.

Selina: I know, I'll end it soon.

Dennis: Good.

Selina: Right after Chinese New Year.

對話譯點通

Selina: 我跟辦公室的同事約會。

Dennis: 妳先生知道嗎？

Selina: 你開玩笑嗎？

Dennis: 怎麼發生的？

Selina: 嗯，就是耶誕派對，我們在會議室碰著，他穿聖誕老公公裝真可愛…

Dennis: 我是說你怎麼會發生那種事。你是個已經結婚了的女人。

Selina: 我知道，但我也只是個女人。

Dennis: 你走在危險邊緣，妳先生如果發現會殺了你。

Selina: 我知道，我會趕緊結束。

Dennis: 這樣最好。

Selina: 農曆年過後。

 單字及片語

see someone	表示跟某人約會，很口語的講法。
uniform	n.制服
Santa uniform	n.聖誕老人裝
thin	adj.薄的
walk on thin ice	走在冰上，表示做危險的事情
find out	v.發現

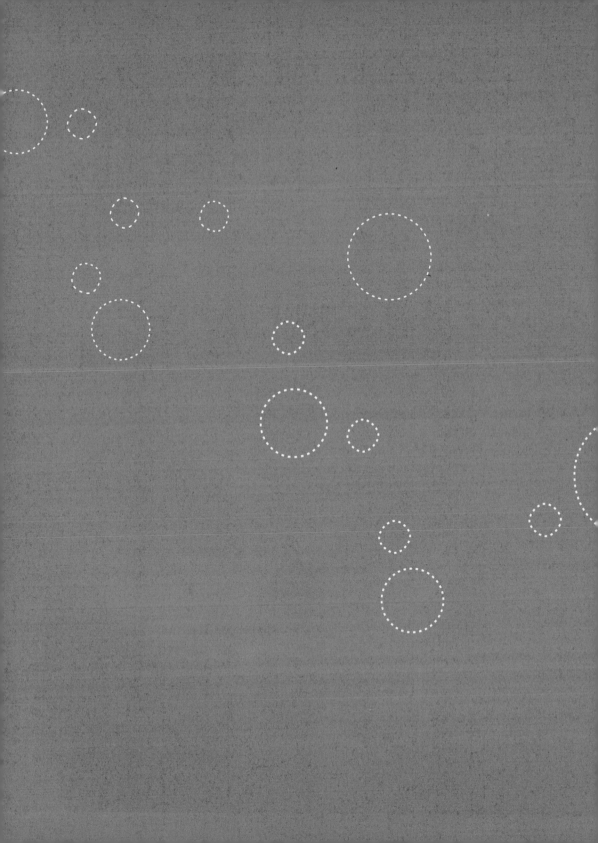

鸚鵡**學**習法

單字 總整理

大家跟我一起唸，一句
唸三遍，學鸚鵡説話就
對了！

♥ 浪漫小語 CD 59

1. **Would you like to go around with me？**
   （要不要跟我在一起？）
2. **Love me a little less, but love me longer.**
   （愛我少一點，但愛我久一點。）
3. **Kiss and make up！**
   （親一下，和好吧！）
4. **The way we were.**
   （往日情懷）
5. **Love is enjoyment；Marriage is tolerance.**
   （愛情是享受，婚姻是忍受。）

♥ 戀愛篇 CD 60

love at first sight	一見鍾情
chat up	搭訕
have a date	約會
first impression	第一印象
excuse	藉口
pub	夜店
harassment	騷擾
dating foreigners	與外國人交往
material girl	拜金女
rich and powerful family	豪門

♥ 熱戀篇 CD 61

pick up	把上、釣（馬子／凱子）
enjoy	享受
living together	同居
on the bed	床上
sweet words	甜言蜜語
giving presents	送禮
long distance relationship	遠距戀情
parking	車震、停車
poetic	詩意的
lovers pledges	海誓山盟

爭吵篇 CD 62

flirt	調情
fight	爭吵
have an affair	劈腿、外遇
cheating	欺騙、偷腥
one-night stand	一夜情
heart-broken	心碎
shackle	桎梏、枷鎖
unfaithful	不忠的
differences of opinion	意見不合
break up	分手

 舊情人篇 CD 63

old flame	舊情人
refreshed memories	往日情懷
second encounter	重逢
How've you been	別來無恙
lovesick	單相思
sticking around	藕斷絲連
dilemma	進退兩難
sex with an ex	和舊情人發生性關係
cute ex	可愛的舊情人
friendship between the opposite sex	異性間的友誼

♥ 修成正果篇 ◎ CD 64

get back together	復合
go steady	穩定交往
propose	求婚
meeting the parents	拜見雙親
shotgun marriage	奉子成婚
inter-racial marriage	異國婚姻
vows	誓言
like husband, like wife	夫妻臉
mistress	情婦
extramarital relationship	婚外情

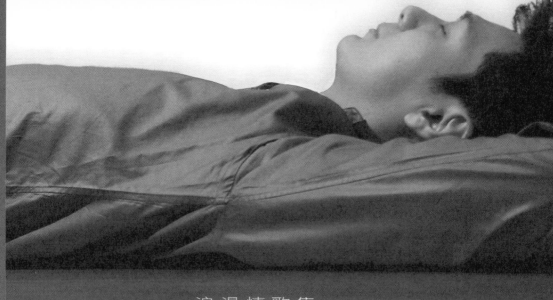

浪漫情歌集

情不自禁

聶 雲 與 烏野薰
爵士樂團

Can't Help Falling in Love
Dennis & Uno Jazz Orchestra

翻開塵封的每段愛情記事
回首模糊的每個熟悉背影

多年後 當愛早已鎖入記憶中
只留下 當年《情不自禁》的感動

如同被愛情磨練得日漸成熟的妳
了解該用何種方式品嚐那些曾經

讓贏雲與UNO用溫柔與浪漫的節奏
陪妳重新回味
那些難忘的《情不自禁》

親愛的 最近好嗎？
還記得當年情不自禁的衝動嗎？
那是愛情中最珍貴甜美的部分啊
而當時我們卻不知道
多年後那是愛情記憶裡僅存的快樂

親愛的 還認得嗎？
這些當年老是惹妳哭的老情歌
現在聽來竟然滿是歡笑的記憶

SANA放空ing

定價：220元
作者：SANA

人氣部落格SANA漫畫網誌首部作品集
2006第二屆『全球華文部落格大獎』決選入圍作品
SANA部落格突破140萬人次，平均每日1萬人上網看SANA網誌
《Taipei walker》、《數位時代》人氣部落格報導
人氣部落創作者：fjumonkey輔大猴、85階公廁OTOKO，大聲推薦！
水瓶鯨魚主辦「I wish」創意漫畫票選大賽，獲『最佳人氣獎』！

人氣部落格圖文創作家SANA的第一部作品，除了收錄SANA網誌上的精華作品外，更有SANA特地為本書所
作、從未公開的精采創作，完整呈現作者獨特的"SA"式幽默---永遠少一根筋、率直單純的脫線喜感。
作品特點包括：爆笑、無厘頭的文字對話 ·俏皮的日式畫風 ·生動的繪圖及貼近生活的故事
全本採用彩色精美印刷，圖像的細緻度與作者的原創性更明顯的表現出來。
《85階公廁》OTOKO、人氣部落格圖文創作者輔大猴 聯合推薦。

《王之道--王建民圖文特輯》(平裝版)

定價：399元
作者：李赫+最堅強棒球達人寫手群

繼《王WANG-王建民榮光全紀錄》之後，時報數位再度推出
WANG王者再現超級大書，有大量精彩圖片，配合名家生動
可讀文字，讓讀者從全新的視角，永久保存王建民！

特點包括：
· 繼《王WANG-王建民榮光全紀錄》震撼市場之後，第二本改寫經典的王建民人物誌。
· 雜誌書、大開本編排，全彩120磅雪銅，大幅圖文走向，極度精緻化，限量珍藏，永久保存版。
· 超級名家執筆，透過各種文體媒材、以多種嶄新角度素就王建民文選。
· 集合最堅強棒球達人寫手群，紐約－台灣跨海佈線，專業分析王建民的球路並預測他的勝投策略。
· 近百張王建民高畫質精彩外電圖片，引自法新社、美聯社等外電，完全收錄王建民每個精采神情動作。
· 直擊紐約洋基球場，貼身記者提供王建民的獨家觀察。

戀愛英文ABC
聶雲：學英文就像談戀愛

作者 / 聶雲 (Dennis Nieh)

採訪整理者 / 楊曉憶 (Yvetee Yang)

編輯主任 / 陳美萍(May Chen)

美術設計 / 簡鳳伶、張雅惠、何怡欣、蔡馥仔

企劃行銷 / 王怡玲

內頁插圖 / 黃淨祺

董事長・發行人 / 孫思照

總經理 / 莫昭平

營運長 / 黃秀錦

副營運長 / 蕭芳祥

編輯總監 / 呂宗熹

業務總監 / 羅斌文

CD錄音 / 聶雲(男聲) Stephanie(女聲)

聶雲照片提供 / 齊石傳播有限公司

出版者 / 時報數位傳播股份有限公司

發行地址 / 108台北市大理街132號

聯絡地址 / 108台北市和平西路三段240號5樓

總經銷 / 時報文化出版企業股份有限公司

讀者服務專線 / 0800-231-705

時報數位官網 / www.onmyown.tw

電子信箱 / onmyown@readingtimes.com.tw

印刷 / 盈昌印刷有限公司

初版一刷 / 2008年2月12日

定價 / 280元

國家圖書館出版品預行編目資料

戀愛英文ABC：聶雲：學英文就像談戀愛／ 聶
雲. 作 - 初版. - 臺北市 ： 時報數位傳播,
2008.02
　　面；　公分
　ISBN 978-986-82910-5-8 (平裝附光碟片)
　1. 英文　2. 會話
805.188　　　　　　　　　　97001332